GHOSTS

TRANSLATED BY CHRIS ANDREWS

CÉSAR AIRA

·

A NEW DIRECTIONS PAPERBOOK ORIGINAL

Originally published as *Los Fantasmas* in 1990; published by arrangement with
the Michael Gaeb Literary Agency, Berlin.

New Directions gratefully acknowledges that the publication of this translation has been
generously assisted with a subvention from TyPA, Buenos Aires, Argentina.

Manufactured in the United States of America
First published as a New Directions Paperbook Original (NDP1133) in 2008

Library of Congress Cataloging-in-Publication Data
Aira, César, 1949–
[Fantasmas. English]
Ghosts / Cesar Aira ; translated from the Spanish by Chris Andrews.
p. cm.
"A New Directions Paperbook Original, NDP1133."
ISBN 978-0-8112-1742-2 (pbk. : alk. paper)
I. Andrews, Chris. II. Title.
PQ7798.1.I7F8313 2008
863'.64—dc22   2008047193

10 9 8 7

New Directions Books are published for James Laughlin
By New Directions Publishing Corporation
80 Eighth Avenue, New York 10011

GHOSTS

ON THE MORNING of the 31st of December, the Pagaldays visited the apartment they already owned in the building under construction at 2161 Calle José Bonifacio, along with Bartolo Sacristán Olmedo, the landscape gardener they had hired to arrange plants on the two broad balconies, front and rear. They climbed the stairs littered with rubble to the middle level of the edifice: like the other apartments, the one they had acquired occupied a whole floor, the fourth. Apart from the Pagaldays there were only six other owners, all of whom made an appearance on that last morning of the year to see how the work was coming along. The builders were conspicuously busy. By eleven, there were people everywhere. It was in fact the day on which, according to the contracts, the apartments should have been ready to move into; but, as usual, there had been a delay. Felix Tello, the construction company's architect, must have gone up and down fifty times, allaying the owners' concerns. Most had come with a tradesman of some kind: a carpet layer to measure the floors, a carpenter, a tiler, or an interior decorator. Sacristán Olmedo was talking about the dwarf palms that would be arranged in rows on the balconies, while the Pagalday children went running through rooms, which still had no flooring, doors or windows. The air conditioning units were being installed, ahead of the elevators, which would have to wait until after the holiday. Meanwhile materials were being hoisted up through the shafts. Perched on their high heels, the ladies were climbing the dusty stairs scattered with pieces of rubble; since the banisters had not yet been fitted, they had to be especially careful. The first basement level was to be used for garages, with ramps up to the street, which had not yet been covered with their special anti-slip surface. The second level was for box rooms and storage space. On top of the seventh floor, a heated swimming pool and a games room, with a panoramic view over rooftops and streets. And the caretaker's apartment, which was no more finished than the rest of the building, but had been inhabited for some months by Raúl Viñas, the night watchman, and his family. Viñas was a reliable Chilean builder, although he had turned out to be a prodigious drinker. The heat was supernatural. Looking down from the top was dangerous. The glass panels that would enclose the whole terrace were not yet in place. The visitors kept their children well away from the edges. It's true that buildings under construction seem smaller before the windows, doors and flooring have been put in. Everyone knows that; and yet somehow the opposite also seemed to be true. Domingo Fresno, the architect in charge of the interiors on the second floor, was walking anxiously through that capacious labyrinth, as if across the sands of a desert. Tello had done his job well enough. At least the building was standing firm on its foundations; it could have melted like an ice cream in the sun. No one had come to see the first floor. The Kahns, an older couple with two young daughters, were on the fifth floor with their decorator, the extraordinary Elida Gramajo, who was calculating aloud, working out the quantities of fabric required for drapes. Every detail had to be taken into account. And no detail could be specified without measuring both the space it would occupy and the surrounding space. Consequently, that big concrete cage was measured exhaustively, in three dimensions, millimeter by millimeter. A woman in violet was catching her breath on the stairs between the sixth and seventh floors. Others didn't have to make an effort: they floated up and down, even through the concrete slabs. The owners were not bothered by the delay, partly because they didn't have to make the last payment until they took possession, but also because they actually preferred to have a bit more time to organize the furnishings and fittings. The measurements were expanding the space that had been shrunken by illusion; similarly, the duration of the move was expanding. Besides, there would have been

something violent about taking possession on the last day
of the year. On the sixth floor, Dorotea and Josefina Itúrbide Sansó, two girls aged five and three, were kicking up
cement dust with their little sandaled feet while their parents chatted placidly with Felix Tello. Tello excused himself
to greet the woman in violet and accompanied her up to
the next floor. They met the Kahns coming down from the
games room and introduced themselves. Meanwhile the
Pagaldays looked out from their balcony at the large plane
trees growing in the Calle Bonifacio. Although not yet fitted with security grilles, the balconies with high balustrades
were, for the moment, the safest place for children. It was a
morning of high childishness. Everything belonged to the
children. The expansion produced by the measurements
and the feeling of contraction that goes with fear were
overlaid by the world of childhood. The real universe is
measured in millimeters, and it is gigantic. Where children
are present, dimensions are always mediated, scaled down.
The decorators were crafting miniatures. Besides, all these
powerful people and this profitable business were operating
for the benefit of the children; if not for them, the parents
would have chosen to live in hotels. Horrible and half-
naked, the builders came and went among them. The fron-
tier between rich and poor, between human beings and
beasts, was a line in time; the space occupied by one group
would soon be taken over by the other. In spite of its symbolism, the 31st was a crude and obvious allusion to this
state of affairs. It was also indisputably true that the poor

had a right to be happy too, and could even exercise that right. The mediation between large and small sums of money is effected by use and especially the diversity of users; possession, on the other hand, is as transitory as the gathering that was taking place that morning on the building site. Fresno was planning to put as many plants inside as Olmedo was putting outside. In a way, they were all landscape gardeners. And indeed, for the time being, the whole site was outside. The building would be finished when it all became an inside. An intimate, armor-plated little universe. Felix Tello himself would vanish like a puff of dust blown away by the passing years. The children would grow up here, for a while at least. The López family, who would occupy the first floor, had small children; they were in their square patio at the back, where the red paving stones had already been laid. The owners of the third floor, who arrived at midday, were the parents of the lady in violet who was going to live up on the seventh; they arrived with her children. There could hardly have been more children; each would have a private landscape, one on top of the other. Ms Gramajo had spent three hours taking notes, writing down figures extracted from space. Mrs De Itúrbide said she had seen a horrible fat monster like a sumo wrestler. He was from Santiago del Estero. A tray with buckets on it was rising up the elevator shaft, hoisted by a little motor. Around one, as the owners were leaving, there was an impromptu meeting on the first floor, where it was cooler. From the top floor you could see into the yard of the police station, which was around the corner, on the Calle Bonorino. An old gentleman, the López's cabinet maker, had measured various walls for bookshelves and cupboards. Since the owners had bought their apartments off a plan, they had all preferred to have their cupboards specially built. The construction company had suggested a firm of cabinet makers who were looking after four floors: their workshops would take orders directly from the decorators. Downstairs, while the parents were talking, various kids watched the workmen filling a big metal dumpster in the street with rubble. They were wheeling their barrows up a sloping plank that was blocking the sidewalk; women coming back from the supermarket on the corner with their trolleys full of provisions for the New Year's Eve feast had to go onto the road, a manoeuvre they accomplished reluctantly. Domingo Fresno was talking with a bearded young architect, an acquaintance of his, who would be doing the interiors on the seventh floor. The moment for swinging into action was, they felt, dizzyingly imminent: although the building seemed utterly incomplete and provisional, with so much rubble and empty space, any day now it could be finished. Elida Gramajo, who had already left, was thinking the same thing. Less mindful of what lay ahead, the owners were thinking something else. But if anyone should have been imagining the disappearance of the builders, seeing them vanish into thin air, without a trace, like bubbles bursting soundlessly, it was them. The electricians stopped working at one on the dot, and left. Tello spoke for a moment with the foreman, then they went to look at the plans, which kept them busy for a good quarter of an hour. Putting in the wiring wouldn't take long at all; the power points and all the rest could be finished off in an afternoon. The parents of the lady in violet climbed up with the children to see the games room on top and the swimming pool, which was already lined with little sky-blue tiles. An extremely thin, badly dressed woman was hanging washing on a line, in what would be the patio of the caretaker's apartment. It was Elisa Vicuña, the night watchman's wife. The visitors looked up at the strange, irregular form of the water tank that crowned the edifice, and the big parabolic dish that would supply television images to all the floors. On the edge of the dish, a sharp metallic edge on which no bird would have dared to perch, three completely naked men were sitting, with their faces turned up to the midday sun; no one saw them, of course. On the fourth floor, the Pagaldays were leafing through the contents of a large oblong portfolio, listening to Sacristán Olmedo's explanations. The children wanted to express their opinions too. Generally, though, what the children wanted was to look out from the balconies: wherever they came from, the difference in height was exciting. Even if they were moving from one third floor to another, there was a difference. What you could see from that height was different. The children were coming up with strange and sometimes illogical ideas about where they were. They resumed their races through the rooms, over the bare cement floors. Light penetrated to the farthest corner. It was as if they were in partitioned fields, raised to a certain height. After exchanging congratulations and best wishes for the year to come with a family that was about to leave, Felix Tello expressed his justifiable confidence that "they would be happy in their new home."

The owners of the apartments had their own idea of happiness; they imagined it wrapped in a delay, a certain developmental slowness, which was already making them happy. In short, they didn't believe that things were going to proceed as planned, that is, quickly. They preferred to think of the gentle slope of events; that was how it had been since they paid the deposit and signed the settlement a year earlier. Why should they adopt a different attitude now, just because the year was coming to an end? True, they knew there would be a change, but at the last moment, beyond all the moments in between. It wouldn't be today, or tomorrow, or any day that could be determined in advance. Like the spectrum of perception, the spectrum of happening is divided by a threshold. That threshold is just where it is, and nowhere else. They were focusing on the year, not the end of the year. Needless to say, they were right, in spite of everything and everyone, even in spite of right and wrong.

The union of the year and the moment was like the ownership of the building. Each owner possessed a floor, a garage and a box room, but nothing else: that was all they could sell. And yet at the same time they owned the whole building. That's how a condominium works.

Standing still on the dumpster's higher side, in the street, was a builder, a young man named Juan José Martínez, with an empty bucket in his hand. He had been distracted by something that had happened on the corner. There was nothing special about the corner or about him. An ordinary sort of guy, who wouldn't normally merit a second glance. Various people looked at him, but only because of where he was standing, perched up there, motionless, looking toward the corner, holding that position for the sheer, childlike pleasure of balancing all on his own in a high place (he was very young). The only unusual thing about him was that stillness, which is rare to see in a person at work, even for a brief spell. It was like stopping movement itself, but without really stopping it, because even in those instants of immobility he was earning wages. Similarly, a statue sculpted by a great master, still as it is, goes on increasing in value. It was a confirmation of the absurd lightness of everything. The people distracted by the sight of him, as he was by the sight of something a certain distance away, knew that future moments of daydreaming would be nourished by the poetic argument they were absorbing, an argument about eternity, about the beyond where promises are set.

The worst thing is the way they lie, Felix Tello was saying, but to judge from the broad smile on his face, he wasn't worried in the least. The architect's words met with a most attentive reception. Such attentiveness is not unusual when the lies of a third party are at issue. Tello was referring to the builders and by extension to the proletariat in general. They lie and lie and lie. Even when they're telling the truth. Enthusiastic up-and-down jerking of heads, to signal assent. Felix Tello was a professional from a middle-class background. From a certain point on in his career, he had associated almost exclusively with two opposite fringes of society: the extraordinarily rich people who bought parts of his sophisticated buildings, and the extremely poor workers who built them. He had discovered that the two classes were alike in many ways, and especially in their complete lack of tact where money was concerned. In that respect the correspondence was exact. The very poor and the very rich regard it as natural to extract the maximum benefit from the person they happen to be dealing with. The middle-class principle, natural to him, of leaving a margin, a ghostly "buffer" of courtesy, between the asking price and the maximum that could be obtained, was foreign to them. Utterly foreign. It didn't even cross their minds. Having associated with both groups for so long, and being both intelligent and adaptable (if that is not a pleonasm), he had learned how to mediate with a fair degree of efficiency. He took advantage of the perfect trap that the rich and the poor had set for each other. Once he had secured the means to sustain a respectably comfortable way of life, all he wanted was to live in peace. The only thing that surprised him, when they confronted each other with their home truths, wearing those stupid expressions, was the sincere perplexity on both sides. It was like the episode in his favorite novel, *L'Assommoir*, in which the heroine, Gervaise, stops paying back the money she owes to the Goujets: "From next month on, I'm not paying you another cent," and soon she even starts charging them for the work she does. What a rude surprise for the bourgeois reader! How could this good, honest, hardworking woman refuse to pay a debt? So what? Why should she pay, just because of some moral obligation? But what about manners? No, manners didn't even come into it, in her situation; she was poor and had an alcoholic husband, and all the rest. That Zola, the man was a genius! (But with this expression, which Tello formulated silently, clasping his hands and lifting his eyes skyward, as if to say "Even I couldn't have come up with that," he un-wittingly confessed that he was fifty thousand times more bourgeois than those who were scandalized by the behavior of the pretty laundress with the limp.)

Except for the oldest couple and the youngest, all the others had embarked on their second, that is to say, defini-tive, marriages. Which is why they had invested in comfort-able, pleasant dwellings, where they could settle down and live for years. That was Tello's style: sensible, child-friendly, family-oriented design. And good business sense, of course.

The little group hanging on his words, those remarried couples with their shared project of happiness, had been infiltrated by two individuals, two naked men covered in fine cement dust. They were listening too, but only as a pretext for bursting continually into fierce, raucous laugh-ter. Or not so much laughter as vehement, theatrically sar-castic howling. Since the others didn't hear or see them, the conversation continued at its polite and leisurely pace.

The naked men shouted louder and louder as if competing with each other. They were dirty like builders, and had the same kind of bodies: rather stocky, solid, with small feet, and rough hands. Their toes were spread widely, like wild men's toes. They were behaving like badly brought-up children. But they were adults. A builder who happened to be passing by with a bucketful of rubble on the way to the skip stretched out his free hand and, without stopping, grasped the penis of one of the naked men and kept walking. The member stretched out to a length of two yards, then three, five, ten, all the way to the sidewalk. When he let it go, it slapped back into place with a noise whose weird harmonics went on echoing off the unplastered concrete walls and the stairs without marble paving, up and down the empty elevator shafts, like the lowest string of a Japanese harp. The two ghosts laughed more loudly and frenetically than ever. The architect was saying that electricians lie, painters lie, plumbers lie.

Most of the visitors were already leaving when a truck loaded with perforated bricks arrived and backed into what would be the lobby on the ground floor. The architect was impressed to see the delivery being made, given the half holiday. He explained to his audience that it was the final load of perforated bricks for partition walls, then indulged in a subtly cruel quip: if anyone wanted to make a last-minute change to the floor plan, they should speak now or forever hold their peace. Things were becoming irrevocable, but that didn't worry the owners; in fact, it enriched their sense of well-being. For the builders, however, the delivery came as an unpleasant surprise, since they had no choice but to unload the truck, and their half-day would have to be extended. They lined up quickly, forming a human chain, as they do for unloading bricks. The two ghosts had taken up a new position in the air above a round-faced electric clock hanging from a concrete beam above the place where the elevator doors would go. Both of them were head-down, with their temples touching; one vertical and the other at an angle of fifty degrees, like the hands of a clock at ten to twelve; but that wasn't the time (it was after one). Tello suggested going upstairs, so as not to get in the way, and to show the late arrivals the games room and the swimming pool, which were the building's prime attractions. Those who were not going up said good bye. When they got to the top, where it was scorchingly hot, they said what a good idea a swimming pool was. The metal skeleton rearing above them required some explanation: the solarium would be roofed with sliding glass panels, moved by a little electric motor, and a special, separate boiler would send hot water through that tangle of pipes, because of course the pool would be used much more in winter than in summer, when people generally go to the beach. A huge number of glass panes had to be fitted: the whole roof and most of the sides (not the south side, facing the street, because that was where the dressing rooms, the bathrooms and the caretaker's apartment would be). The laminated glass, with an interlayer of pure crystal, had already been delivered; the packages were waiting in the basement. The fitting of the panes would be one of the last jobs. They went to the edge to look at the view. It wasn't truly panoramic (after all, they were only at seventh-floor level), but it was fairly sweeping, and took in the impressive rampart of buildings along the Avenida Alberdi, with its crazy racing traffic, a hundred yards away, plus a broad expanse of houses and gardens, and a few scattered high-rise buildings in the distance. And overhead a glorious dome of sky, the cobalt blue of summer midday. Except in the early morning, the sun would be visible from the pool all day long. As they had noticed a number of children watching them, they started talking about the night watchman and his family. News of his drinking had reached them, but it was not a cause for worry: the proximity of the police station, which they could see from where they were, had insured them against theft during the construction of the building, in spite of the watchman's distractedness and hangovers. Within a few weeks, the family would be gone. They're Chileans, did you know? Yes, they had thought so. Chileans were different: smaller, more serious, more orderly. And in the architect's experience they were also respectful, diligent, excellent workers. Naturally Raúl Viñas was in the habit of getting drunk with his Chilean relatives, some of whom had been employed as laborers on the site. Very soon they would all disappear forever, them and the others. They had been living on the site for a year. The owners found all this curiously soothing. Someone had to be living there before they came to live definitively. They could even imagine the happiness of being there, provisionally, balancing on the edge of time. During the first months, while the frame went up, the night watchman's family had lived on the ground floor in a very flimsy shelter with cardboard walls, then they came up to the top. In a way it was a rather poetic existence, but it must have been terribly cold for them in winter, and now they were roasting. Not that Raúl Viñas cared, of course. And, naturally, they had lied: for a start, they weren't legal residents; they didn't have work permits. On the other hand, they were paid practically nothing, although it was a lot for them, because of the exchange rate. Apparently they already had somewhere to live afterward, and in fact they'd been asked to stay a few weeks more, because it wasn't worth hiring another night watchman for such a short time. "They're better off than us," said Mrs De López. At least as far as timing was concerned, they agreed.

Meanwhile, on the third floor, the carpet layer, a short, chubby man, was checking his notes for the last time, room by room, and sometimes taking the measurements again, just to be sure that he hadn't made a mistake. After reading off the number, he flicked his wrist expertly and the metal tape retracted itself, dancing about briskly, making a sheathing noise. All the measurements were right. All of them, from the first to the last. He could have carpeted the ceilings. Before going down, he leant over the balcony to see if his mini-van, a yellow Mitsubishi, was still where he had parked it. Directly below him the snout of a big truck was sticking out, the truck from which the bricks were being unloaded.

The builders were in such a hurry they had made two chains instead of one. Eight of them were busily at work. Two men in the back of the truck took the perforated bricks three at a time and threw them down to a pair below, who threw them in turn to two more builders, who threw them on to the last pair, who piled them up against a wall. Each flight of the bricks through the air was the same as the previous flights, down to the way they separated slightly and were clapped back together in the hands of the catcher, making a sound like castanets. People with time on their hands are often fascinated by the sight of this operation and spend hours watching from the opposite sidewalk. In this case the only spectator was a fat little four-or five-year old boy with blond hair, who had walked in beside the truck. After watching the synchronized movements for a few minutes, he approached Raúl Viñas, who was juggling bricks in one of the chains, and asked him: Aren't the kids here, Mister? Viñas, who was in a particularly bad mood because lunch had been delayed, didn't even look at him. It seemed he wouldn't answer, but then he did, with a mono-syllable, through the smoke of his cigarette (he was manag-ing to smoke while catching and throwing bricks, three by three): No. The kid insisted: Are they upstairs? Another silence, bricks going and coming, and the boy: Huh? Finally Viñas said: José María, why don't you fuck off home? The builders burst out laughing. Offended, José María stepped aside and stood there watching, quite calmly. Offended, but pleased that his name had been pronounced. Besides, he really was interested in Operation Bricks. He was in no hurry, because lunch was late at his place, and anyway, he always waited until his grandmother, a little old lady with a powerful voice, whose shouts had made his name known throughout the neighborhood, came to fetch him (she lived around the corner). But then he saw one of the naked individuals, white with cement dust, at the back of the building, and went tearing out the way he had come in. The fat guy from Santiago del Estero on the back of the truck, dripping sweat as he heaved the bricks, remarked: How strange. Which made the others laugh again, partly because of his accent and partly just to prolong the fun. They laughed mechanically, without losing concentration, which was all that mattered until the job was done.

Meanwhile, Raúl Viñas' young nephew, Abel Reyes, was at the supermarket on the corner buying provisions for the builders' lunch. As usual, he was keeping it simple and quick: meat, bread, fruit. As youths of a certain age often do, he refused to use the shopping trolleys provided, and since he didn't have bags either, he was carrying everything in his arms. Barely out of childhood, he wasn't really a youth yet. Although fifteen years old, he looked eleven. He was thin, ugly, awkward, and his hair was very long. On arriving in Argentina with his parents two years earlier, he had been struck by the way young men wore their hair long, as common in the new country as it was rare back home: he

thought it was sublime. Being young, foreign and therefore
naïve, he didn't realize that the Argentineans with long hair
belonged to the lowest social stratum, and were precisely
those who had condemned themselves never to escape from
it. But even if he had realized, it wouldn't have mattered to
him. He liked the look, and that was that. So he let his hair
grow; it already reached half way down his back, below his
flat shoulder blades. It looked truly awful. His parents, who
were humble, decent people, had unfortunately tried to reason him out of it; if they had threatened him or issued a de-
cree, he would have submitted to the scissors straight away.
But no, they began by telling him he looked like a girl, or
a lout; and once they had set off on that path, there was no
end to it. They couldn't retract their reasoning, which was
sound. Besides, they were kind and understanding. They said:
"He'll get over it." Meanwhile their son went around looking like a little woman. Since his hair got in the way when
he was working, he had thought of putting it in a pony tail
with an elastic band, but for the moment he didn't dare. On
the building sites no one remarked on it, or even deigned
to notice. It really was very common; at least he had been
right about that. In Chile, he would have been interviewed
on television or, more likely, thrown into prison.

The supermarket was bustling. It was peak hour, on a
peak day. The place had been seized by a buying frenzy.
People were stripping the shelves bare, to make sure they
wouldn't run out of food on New Year's Eve. In the freez-
ers down at the back, he was lucky to find two big packets

of beef ribs, which chilled his hands. He was also carrying a bunch of grilling sausages, a rib cap roast folded into four, and twelve steaks, all sitting in little white trays and wrapped in transparent plastic film. He went to the fruit section and chose two small bags of peaches that seemed to be fairly ripe, and a dozen bananas. All this was complicated to carry without a bag. And the worst was still to come. Before getting the bread he went to look at the ice creams, which were in a deep, trough-like refrigerator. There would have been no point getting ice cream, of course, because it would have melted well before the time came to eat it; but those eight-serve tubs of butterscotch would have been perfect. Two of them would have done the job. He decided to tell his uncle: maybe someone could come back for them at the appropriate moment. It was risky, though, because everything was getting snapped up. He could only hope that the price would put people off; it was very high, after all. Now, yes, the bread. It was essential not just as an accompaniment, but also for resting the meat on, country-style. To eat like that you need a very sharp knife, so to keep their blades honed they were always having to call one of those knife sharpeners who go around blowing on flutes (except that the man who worked in that neighborhood used an ocarina: he must have been the only one in Buenos Aires). Every day, Abel was annoyed by the way they only sold bread in small loaves, barely nine ounces. Four of those little loaves in plastic bags went on top of the packets of meat and the fruit, making a precarious pile; they kept slipping off. But what could he do, short of making two trips? Like a father carrying a big baby in his arms, he headed for the drinks section. Unfortunately, since there was no refrigerator on the site, the builders had to do without cold drinks. But you got used to it, the way you get used to all sorts of things. Abel took two big plastic bottles of Coca-Cola, picking them up by the tops with the index finger and thumb of each hand, which was all he had free. The shoppers had increased considerably in number, and movement along the aisles was obstructed by the supermarket employees, who had begun to mop the floor. Abel looked rather out of place among the other clients, with his torn shirt and long hair, holes in his shoes and cement dust on his trousers. It was amazing how skinny he had stayed, with all the strenuous physical work he had to do. At first glance you could have mistaken him for a girl, a little housemaid. His heart sank when he saw the checkout queue: it stretched the full length of the supermarket, about thirty yards, down to the back, around the corner, and all the way up the next aisle to the front again. Although there were three checkouts, only one was in operation today, and the woman operating it was extremely incompetent; even Abel, who was notoriously dopey, had realized that. In fact, the whole supermarket worked in an inefficient and rather arbitrary way. It wasn't run as a commercial enterprise; its aim in serving the clients wasn't to make a profit but to do something else, something religious, though what exactly wasn't clear. It was part of a chain that belonged to an evangelical sect; you could tell by the lack of business sense. Or rather, you could tell by considering any aspect of the supermarket, right down to the finest details, since the whole place was pervaded by the quintessence of the ineffable: religion. It was rumored that attempts were made to indoctrinate young workers from the neighborhood who happened to venture into the supermarket: they were accosted and presented with a videocassette showing the finest performances of the sect's patriarch, a North American pastor. Abel Reyes had not been accosted, although he was the only young worker who went there every day: either they had picked him for a Chilean, and therefore a die-hard, fanatical Catholic, or decided he wasn't much of a catch, because of his hair and what it suggested about his character, or, perhaps, they had thought he wouldn't have a video player at home (or that he didn't know English and wouldn't be able to understand the sermons). He went to the end of the queue, slightly hunched, as always, and started moving forward little by little. It was then that he saw his aunt with the children.

It was getting on for midday, a fateful hour for the house-wife, and up in the solar oven, Elisa Vicuña was needled by the feeling that the supermarket on the corner, her sole source of provisions, on which she depended absolutely, might shut at twelve: it wouldn't have been surprising, not only because most people were taking half the day off, but also because that supermarket was unpredictable; it could be shut already, or it could stay open till five to midnight. Now, if it was shut, she was in trouble, because she hadn't done even half the shopping for the celebrations that night; so she decided to go and check, although she hadn't planned to do so, in order to avoid a catastrophic surprise. She tried to go on her own, to save time, but the children simply refused to stay with Patri, who she was leaving in charge of the food while she was gone. She had to put shoes on the barefooted ones, and since some of them hadn't even washed their faces and wouldn't cooperate, it took her fifteen minutes to make them more or less presentable (combing their hair and so on). She would never get used to those stairs without banisters, covered with rubble, stones and dust. She carried the baby girl in her arms and the others went down on their own, leaping about, but none of them had ever fallen. There were four children, two boys and two girls; the oldest (a boy) was seven and the youngest (the baby girl) was almost two. She thought they were very pretty, and no doubt they were, with something of their father's manner, and something from their mother's side as well. Elisa was a lady of thirty-five, slim and rather short (slightly shorter than her husband, who wasn't tall), and naturally, given the family's economic status, not very elegantly dressed or presented. On the first floor, where she noticed that the visitors who had been wandering around the site all morning had disappeared, she exchanged a few words with her husband. Then she left, with the children in tow. She made the baby girl walk, which meant she had to go very slowly. The supermarket was just down the street, no more than thirty yards away, on the same side. Still, it was an outing. As always, the children went running around the columns of the brick façade along the side of the supermarket.

As soon as she reached the door she was stunned by the number of people inside. She might have foreseen something similar (although she wasn't given to such predictions), but not so many people, or even half as many. Reality usually outstrips predictions, even if no one has made them. All she could do was remind herself why she had come: to check if they were shutting at midday. Since there was no notice to be seen, she went in to ask. At the counter where they gave coupons in exchange for containers, ten people were waiting, all carrying huge loads of empty bottles and complaining; there was no one to serve them. The kids had already gone down the aisles, as they always did, and disappeared into the crowd. Unruffled, their mother went to look for them, and find someone to ask while she was at it. Elisa Vicuña was that anomaly, not nearly as rare as is often supposed: a mother immune to the terrifying fantasy of losing her children in a crowd. Reality kept proving her right, since she always found them again, if they were ever lost in the first place. She was still holding the baby girl, Jacqueline, by the hand. In the first aisle she went down, threading her way among trolleys and shoppers, she came across the boy who usually served at the bottle counter; he was mopping the floor, with great difficulty because of all the people coming and going. She was relieved when he told her that they would be shutting at four. That meant she could come back after lunch. She continued in her search for the children, looking at packets of food on the way. She was trying to make a mental list. She had to pick up Jacqueline, who had started to whine, and then wanted to get down again as soon as she saw the other kids. The three of them were standing in front of a supermarket employee in a red apron, wearing too much make up, who was handing out little sample cups of coffee to anyone willing to try them. The kids obviously wanted to ask for some, but they didn't dare; she wouldn't have given them any, of course, and they didn't even know what it was. They had never tasted coffee. But they had been overcome by childish curiosity, that craving to receive. Since she was there in the supermarket, Elisa took a bottle of bleach off the shelf, thinking she had run out, or was about to. She consumed a great deal of bleach, because she used it for all her washing. It was a habit of hers. Which explained why all the family's clothes were so faded and had that threadbare look, humble and worn and yet beautifully so. Even if an article of clothing was new, or brightly colored when she bought it, from the very first wash (a night-long soak in bleach) it took on the whitish, delicate and somehow aristocratic appearance that distinguished the clothes of the Viñas family. As soon as she picked up the bottle, however, she realized how absurd it would be to queue for an hour to buy just that; she would go straight to the checkout and ask the person at the head of the queue to let her in, since she only had one item. She gathered the children and told them it was time to go. Whether out of obedience or boredom, they followed. But as it turned out, she didn't even have to go through with the manoeuvre, which often caused a fuss if there happened to be one of those argumentative women at the head of the queue, because she spotted her nephew Abel near the other end, with his arms full of packets and the two big bottles of Coke hanging from his fingers. Poor thing: what an ugly, ridiculous-looking kid, with his hair falling all over his shoulders. He had seen her too, and greeted her from a distance with his polite little smile, reserved, of course, for members of the family. She came over and asked him to do her a favor: buy the bleach (she gave him an austral from her purse) and then bring it up to her. Abel accepted graciously. She looked at what he had bought, and judged it to be insufficient. Tactlessly, she told him so, leaving him there downcast and worried, with the bottle of bleach on the floor, between his feet. Off they went. On the way out, the kids ran into José María on his bicycle. They pleaded raucously with their mother to let them stay and play on the sidewalk for a while, especially the older boy, Juan Sebastián, to whom José María was going to lend the bike. But she took a firm stand, because, as she said, "it was already time for lunch." That little brat was always hanging around in the street. She didn't want to have to come down again in half an hour to look for them. They went on whining, interminably, and in the end she spent fifteen minutes on the corner, talking to the florist, while they ran around. When she went up, dragging the children with her, there was still no sign of her nephew with the bleach.

Abel Reyes was still queuing patiently; his arms had gone numb from the weight. There were some very pretty girls in the queue, and he was watching them to pass the time. But in the most discreet way. He could truthfully have said that girls were what he liked best in the world, but he always admired them from a certain distance, held back by his pathological, adolescent shyness. He also felt that the inevitable stillness of a supermarket queue put him at a disadvantage. Movement was his natural state, albeit the movement of flight. To him, stillness seemed a temporary exception. He advanced step by step, as the train of full trolleys made its very slow way forward. Many of them were full to capacity, with what looked like provisions for a whole year. The people behind and ahead of him in the queue were talking continually. He was the only one who was silent. He couldn't believe that the neutron bomb really existed. Here, for example, how could it eliminate people and not things, since they were so inextricably combined? In a situation like this, a supermarket queue, things were extensions of the human body. Still, since he had nothing better to do, he imagined the bomb. A silent explosion, lots of radiation. Would the harmful radiation get into the packets of food, the boxes and tins? Most likely. An analogy for death by neutron bomb occurred to him: you're at home, listening to the radio, and a song begins to play; then you go out, and you hear the same song coming from the window of a house down the street. A block further on, a car drives past with the song playing on its radio. You catch a bus, the radio is on, and what do you hear but the same song, still going—without meaning to, you've practically heard it all. Everyone hears the radio (at some point during the day) and many people have it tuned in to the same station. For some reason this struck him as an exact analogy, supernaturally exact; only the effects were different. These thoughts helped him to while away the time. As usual, the trolleys just in front of him took longer than the others; the woman at the checkout even went to the bathroom and left them standing there for ten extra minutes. But everything comes to pass. Finally, it was his turn. It was a relief to put his shopping down on the metal counter. The cashier pressed the wrong buttons on the electronic register a couple of times, as she had done with almost all the clients. Every time she made a mistake she had to call the supervisor, who pushed through the hostile multitude and used a key to cancel the error. It came to forty-nine australs. Abel paid with a fifty-austral note, and the cashier asked if he didn't have any change. He rummaged in his pockets, but of course he had no change, not a cent. The note he had given her was all the money he had brought. The cashier hesitated, looking grief-stricken. Don't you? she asked. She stared as if urging him to check. Abel had noticed that the cashiers at this supermarket (maybe it was the same everywhere) made a huge fuss about change. They always had plenty, but they still made a fuss. In this case there was really no reason: she only had to give him one austral. He was waiting, holding the one-austral note his aunt had given him, folded in four. The cashier looked at the note. So that she could see it wasn't hiding forty-eight others, Abel unfolded it for her. In the end she lifted the little metal clip holding down the one-austral notes in the register (there were at least two hundred), extracted one with utter disgust, ripped off the receipt and handed it over without even looking at him. He went straight for the door, forgetting his shopping, which was still on the counter. The woman behind him in the queue, who had started to pile her purchases on top of his, called out: Why did you pay for this stuff if you don't want to take it away? Back he came, mortally embarrassed, and gathered it all up as best he could. He dropped the little loaves of bread, and various other things. By the time he got back to the site, the truck had gone, and they were waiting for him with the fire alight under the grill. His uncle and another builder, an Argentinean named Aníbal Fuentes, or Aníbal Soto (curiously, he was known by both names), who were the designated grillers, tossed the meat onto the grill, a rectangular piece of completely black wire mesh. What's that? Viñas asked him, pointing at the bottle of bleach. It's for Auntie Elisa, Abel replied, I'll just take it up to her. They asked him to get some things while he was there, glasses and so on. He disappeared up the stairs. Since the architect had left, Viñas decided to close up the wooden fence, and put the chain on, but not the lock. Now, at last, they could have their lunch in peace.

It's strange that they hadn't bought any wine, isn't it? Especially since some of the men were committed winedrinkers. But there were two reasons why the builder's young butler hadn't even thought of buying any: first, they didn't drink wine at lunchtime as a rule, except occasionally on a Saturday, when as well as knocking off early they had something to celebrate, like a birthday. The second reason was that Raúl Viñas bought all the wine himself at a store in the neighborhood, where they had a special bottling system, and recycled the bottles over and over, which worked out to be very practical and cheap. He had already laid in provisions for that day, and for the next day as well. It was an extra special occasion: for a start, they were stopping work early, so they could drink their fill if they wanted to. Afterward they would be going to their respective homes to get ready for the party that night, a big family do. There was also something to celebrate, of course, because it was the end of the year. Overall it had been a memorable year, a year of work and relative prosperity; they couldn't complain about that. It could even have been called a year of happiness, although not straight away; they would have to wait some time for that to become apparent, in retrospect. It wasn't over yet: there were ten hours left, to be precise. So Raúl Viñas was keeping fourteen bottles of red wine cool, with a system he had invented, or rather discovered, himself. It consisted of resolutely approaching a ghost and inserting a bottle into his thorax, where it remained, supernaturally balanced. When he went back for it, say two hours later, it was cold. There were two things he hadn't noticed, however. The first was that, during the cooling process, the wine came out of the bottles and flowed like lymph all through the bodies of the ghosts. The second was that this distillation transmuted ordinary cheap wine, fermented in cement vats, into an exquisite, matured cabernet sauvignon, which not even captains of industry could afford to drink every day. But an undiscriminating drinker like Viñas, who chilled his red wine in summer just because of the heat, wasn't going to notice the change. Besides, he was accustomed to the wonderful wines of his country, so it seemed perfectly natural to him. And, indeed, what could be more natural than to drink the best wines, always and only the best?

When Abel Reyes reached the top floor (curiously, climbing the stairs never seemed to cost him any effort: he let his mind wander, and before he knew it, he was there) he found his uncle's children in the middle of their lunch. The caretaker's apartment had been minimally fitted out, ahead of the rest of the building, to make it livable for Viñas and his family. But not much had been done, just the bare minimum. No tiles on the floor, no plaster on the ceiling, or paint on the walls; no fittings in the bathroom, or glass in the windows. But there was running water (although it hadn't been running for long), and electricity from a precariously rigged-up cable. That was all they needed. There were two medium-sized rooms, plus the kitchen and bathroom. All the furniture was borrowed and rudimentary. The children were sitting around a homemade table, with chops and peas on their plates. They didn't want to eat, of course. In front of Patri were four glasses, a bottle of soda water, and a carton of orange juice. She was looking severely at her half-siblings, who were looking at the glasses and whimpering. The idea was to make them understand that unless they ate, they wouldn't get anything to drink. They were dying of thirst, they said. Their mother was making macaroons in the kitchen, and had switched off for the moment. Patri, being younger, had more patience; in fact, since she was still a child in some ways, she was patient to a fault, and rose to the children's challenge, refusing to yield a drop. Trying all their options with a wicked cunning, they cried out to their mother. But Elisa didn't respond, not just because she was in the kitchen; her mind was elsewhere. All of a sudden Patri filled the glasses with juice and soda and distributed them. The children drank eagerly. She finished her chop and peas, and had a drink as well. The baby girl, sitting by her side, wanted to leave the table. Patri picked her up and began to spoon-feed her. The others started getting rowdy. Juan Sebastián, the eldest, had eaten more than the others, but still not finished his meal. The older girl, Blanca Isabel, hadn't even started, and was already asking for more to drink. The heat in the dining room was intense, but the light was very mild, because the window was covered with a piece of cardboard. The sun was beating on the cardboard, which was thick, but seemed to be slightly translucent. That summer light is incredibly strong.

What could you do to cool off up there? Well, nothing.

It was pure heat, perfectly real and concrete. Beyond the shadow of a doubt. And yet, if not shored up by eternities of faith, it would have crumbled to a puff of ice-dust. Having drunk a glass of soda water and juice, not so much because she was thirsty, but to set an example for the children, Patri was suddenly covered in perspiration. Blanca Isabel, who didn't miss a thing, said, Did you go for a dip? Thinking it wouldn't have such a spectacular effect, Patri helped herself to another glass. Feeling she had done it to taunt them, Juan Sebastián leapt to his feet and ran to the kitchen to tell his mother, who paid him no attention. They all started crying out for more to drink. You'll have to make do with tap water, because that's all there is left, said Patri, showing them the remaining soda. She gathered up the glasses again to make orangeade, with the dregs, in equal quantities, but only for those who would eat. They made an effort, and she even had to cut the remains of Ernesto and Blanca Isabel's chops into little pieces. Elisa looked out and asked if they had finished. The meat, said Patri, but not the peas. Sebastián was the only one who had polished off his meal, but what a performance it had been. His mother asked him if he wanted any more. He replied with a groan: he had eaten so much, he was full, stuffed. Patri distributed the glasses. The children emptied them in the blink of an eye. She left Jacqueline on her chair and went to the kitchen to get the grapes. It's the same every day, she said to Elisa: they just don't want to eat. It's because of the heat, Elisa replied, poor things. She asked Patri if she wanted to finish the peas. Echoing the children, she said she couldn't. But wasn't Elisa going to have anything? She hadn't even sat down. No, she said, she wasn't hungry. Although, in the end, she ate the plate of leftover peas, because she hated to waste them. Patri went back into the dining room with the grapes and a clean knife, with which she cut them in half and took out the seeds. Each child received one grape at a time, and Jacqueline's took a bit longer, because she had to remove the skin as well. Luckily she was good with her hands.

Abel went straight to the kitchen and put the bottle of bleach on the bench for his aunt. There was a big skylight in the ceiling, and at that hour of the day, the sun was shining straight into it. Elisa had covered it with a blue towel, which had been wet for a while. That might have afforded some protection from the heat, but in any case it was stifling, especially since she had been cooking. She asked Abel if he was going to stay and eat with the men. Well I'm not going to leave now, am I, he said, as if it were obvious. Have you told your mother? No, he hadn't, why? Because she'll be expecting you, she said. It hadn't occurred to him. But Abel said he didn't think she would, since he hadn't told her about the half-holiday. She might have worked that out for herself, said Elisa. I don't think so, I don't think so, said Abel impatiently. His aunt didn't really know his mother, he thought. She didn't realize that his mother didn't look after him the way she looked after her children, or even her nieces and nephews. Like all adolescents, he believed that any family was preferable to his own. The belief was

entirely unfounded, but he held it all the same. Elisa had
guessed all this, and let it pass. She asked him who they had
invited for the New Year celebrations. Abel replied: his elder
brother's girlfriend and her family. And he launched into
a detailed description of those potential relatives, making
them out to be the epitome of all the virtues and pow-
ers. His brother's future brother-in-law had an auto-repair
shop, and Abel liked to portray him as a big shot, someone who could do just what he liked, whatever took his
fancy, because he had the means. He ran through a detailed
catalogue of the big shot's properties, exaggerating outrageously. Because of some subtle bias in the subject, or sub-
jects in general, property led on to food. Abel believed that
he had very special tastes, worthy of careful study, without
which they might seem a mere jumble of preferences. Elisa
let him go on, but her mind soon wandered. There was no
point feeling too sorry for him just because he was ugly
and stupid. She made a suggestion: it would be best not to
drink wine at lunch. They're all going to end up trashed,
those animals, she said. I never drink wine, said Abel, with
a characteristic lack of tact (he was speaking to the wife of
the biggest drunk in the family!). When Patri came in to get
the grapes, they greeted each other with a kiss. She thought
he was ridiculous, but was quite fond of him. They always
laughed about him behind his back, because of his hair. Her
hair and his were the same length, and even the same kind:
slightly coarse, straight and black. When the girl went out,
he chatted on and on with Elisa, until, fed up, she told him

to go down, because the men would probably have started eating already.

When they had finished the grapes, the children escaped, without shoes, and went to play in the empty swimming pool, which was in full sun. But they loved it, almost as if the pool were full and they were splashing about in cool water. The three older children were always playing make-believe adventure games, and the baby girl tagged along. She was always there, and was sometimes useful, as a victim, for example, a role that didn't require much skill, or none at all. After various days of other scenarios, they had returned to car racing. They had a number of little plastic cars. Their childish instincts had alerted them to the silence below, where the builders had stopped working, so they ventured down the stairs to the sixth floor, and then to the fifth. The cars went down the stairs in little hands and parked in the farthest rooms. Excited to have the whole building to themselves, or at least the upper floors, the children complicated their game, leaving a car on one floor and going down to the next, then coming back up to look for it, taking unfamiliar routes. A building site was the least appropriate place for a car race (although ideal for hide and seek), and yet the adverse conditions made the game special, giving it a novel, impossible flavor, which made them forget everything else. They felt they had gone straight to the heart of truth or art. Jacqueline kept getting lost and crying. Ernesto, who was specially attached to her, went to the rescue, up or down, depending on where he was. The only interruption occurred when Abel said, Careful not to fall, and continued on his way down to the ground floor. When he was two floors below them, they began to call out "Mophead!" Then they resumed their game with the toy cars, going up and down. A breeze was blowing over those superposed platforms, but it was slight and not very refreshing; in any case the heat would probably begin to ease off once the sun began to go down. The light must have been changing, gradually, but it wasn't noticeable; the brightly-colored toy cars were the light-meters in the children's game. They went down to the third floor, but didn't dare go any further, because they could hear the men's voices.

All the builders had, in fact, gone downstairs a fair while before, and since they wouldn't be returning to work, had washed and changed, to make themselves more comfortable for lunch. The radicals among them had hosed themselves down and dried off in the sun, out in the back yard. They had taken off their work clothes, which, once shed, were so many dusty, torn and mended (or not even mended) rags, and packed them away in their bags. Clean now, hair combed, they sat down around a table made of planks to wait for lunch. They had put the table as far away as possible from the grill, where Aníbal Soto was checking on the progress of the meat. There were ten of them in all. As well as Viñas and Reyes, there were two other Chileans: Enrique Castro and Felipe Rojas. Rojas was known as Pocketman because he was in the habit of keeping his hands in his pockets, even when he was sitting down. It was a pretext for endless jokes. Now, for example, he was sitting with a glass in his left hand and his right hand in his pocket. Next to him was the fat guy from Santiago del Estero, who although by no means an ingenious joker, could get a laugh by dint of sheer ingenuity. He put his hand into the Chilean's pocket to find out what was so nice in there, as he put it. This made all the others laugh, and gave Pocketman a start, making him spill a few drops of wine, which he complained about. The master builder, a short man with grey hair and blue eyes (he was Italian) was convulsed with laughter, but he knew how to change the subject in time. They had all served themselves a glass of wine and were drinking it as an aperitif. Luckily it was cool down there; it was almost like having air conditioning. They drank a toast, and so on. The meat was soon ready, but they had clean forgotten to make a salad. Reproachful gazes converged on young Reyes, who almost always forgot to buy something or other. But, since it was the last day of the year, it didn't matter. Anyway, the meat was first-class.

As well as the Chileans, there was another foreigner, a Uruguayan called Washington Mena; he was an insignificant person, without any noteworthy characteristics. The other one with long hair was a young Argentinean, about twenty, called Higinio Gómez (Higidio, actually, but he said Higinio because it was less embarrassing), who was spectactularly ugly: he had what used to be called a "pock-marked" face, due in fact to a case of chronic acne, as well as that long hair, almost as long as Abel's, but curly. Then there was one they called The Bullshit Artist behind his back, although his name was Carlos Soria. While the others laughed at the fat guy's joke, he just mumbled and ended up making openly sarcastic remarks. The joker from Santiago del Estero turned out to be the most curious character of them all, partly, in fact mainly, because he was spherically fat. That transformed him. He also fancied himself as a wit and even a Don Juan. His name was Lorenzo Quincata; he spoke very little and always gave careful consideration to what he was going to say, but even so, no one would have mistaken him for an intelligent young man.

Soria started running down Santiago del Estero and its inhabitants. They let him talk, but teased him all the while. He said that in Santiago they drank hot beer. Really? How come? He'd been there, of course, passing through; nothing could have persuaded him to stay on those sweltering plains. One day, in a bar, he had sampled that strange beverage (strange for him, anyway). They used a wheelbarrow to bring the beer in from the yard, where it had been sitting in full sun; it was hot like soup, he said. Someone asked him: Why the wheelbarrow? To bring the cartons in, of course, what else could they use? How many cartons, they asked, suspecting him of exaggerating. First he said thirty-six, then he said eight, but it wasn't really clear which number he meant. He pointed out that there had been twenty people drinking. Some of the builders were laughing so hard they cried. That'd have to be a record, wouldn't it, they said. If he drank thirty-six cartons of hot beer all on his own.

Only in Santiago del Estero . . . , said Raúl Viñas, laughing too. He clinked his glass with Quincata. Viñas was a Santiago man himself, he explained, but from Santiago de Chile, which made all the difference.

Soria pointed out once again that there were twenty people drinking, a whole team of road workers. The cartons of bottles were sitting in the yard, out in the sun. Did they know what his belly was like, after drinking it? Well, round, of course. As for how it felt, best not to imagine that, or even try. And yet they did.

Castro reminded Viñas about a famous liar they had known in Chile, a man who, whenever he met someone, would say that that he had just crossed the Andes from Argentina, braving extremely risky or at least unusual conditions, coming through unlikely passes, or right over the mountain peaks, crossing snowfields, always on foot, alone, setting off on the spur of the moment. Each time he ran into someone he knew, he came out with the same story, or rather, a variation. But sometimes he ran into the same person again quite soon afterward, and then he had to invent the opposite journey, since he couldn't always be crossing from Argentina into Chile, without crossing back the other way at least occasionally, indeed just as often, even in the world of the imagination with its somewhat flexible laws. It was a pretext for doubling his lies.

"Lorenzo", they felt, was an incongruous name. They all

thought it suited its owner, but at the first stirring of doubt, they flipped over to the opposite opinion. It was the same with "Washington," and again with "Higinio," and so on through the names, even the commonest ones, like "Abel," "Raúl" and "Juan." It would have been absurd to claim that people looked like examples of their names, and yet, in a curious way, they did. The worst (or the best) thing was that in any given case you could convince yourself of a name's appropriateness or inappropriateness simply by listening to the other person's arguments, and if that became the norm, even within a small community of friends or colleagues, it would be like seeing ghosts emerge. They were pouring out wine for familiar ghosts. (The real ones had disappeared a while before, as they did every day when the smell of meat rose from the grill, as if it were detrimental to them. But they would reappear later on, more active than ever, at siesta time, which was the high point of their day, in summer at least; in winter, it was dusk.)

This reminded the master builder of certain regrettable episodes from the past; some of the men present had been working with him for quite a few years, and they joined in the reminiscing. There was the time they had put up a building, like this one, or even bigger, with materials and tools that were hopelessly inadequate, especially the tools. You know the way there's always some liar exaggerating outrageously, he said. Well, it was really like that. But in this case, the witnesses, including Carlitos Soria (The Bullshit Artist), were not going to let him get away with lying.

Which building? they asked him. The one on Quintino Bocayuva. Oh, that one! They all remembered how terrible it had been. Torture. Instead of ... just about everything, really, they had had to make do with, well, anything at all, whatever came to hand. Instead of wheelbarrows, they used some old baby carriages they found dumped in a vacant lot. Instead of buckets, flowerpots (they had to block up the hole in the bottom). And it was the same with everything else: a truly abject scramble for makeshift solutions, which had scarred them for life.

In less than an hour, and the time flew by because of the interesting conversation, every last mouthful of food disappeared, including the bananas and the peaches and the bread. There was really nothing strange about that: the whole idea was to eat it up. With the wine, however, it was different. In a sense, drinking it was not the whole idea. And yet that is what they had been doing, and they continued: instead of coffee after the meal, they had a glass of wine, or two. The drinking, in fact, had become absolute. Inevitably, though, some drank more than others. The three adult Chileans (young Abel Reyes was drinking Coca-Cola) were the quickest, and so attained the highest level of stupefaction, to the point where they could hardly say a coherent good-bye when the others began to leave. And yet they still had some more drinking to do. They did it sitting down, staring into space, smiling vaguely. The others finally vanished, and the three of them underwent a kind of collapse. They felt as if they had imbibed the whole world, but in tiny doses, or as if a joy outside of them had begun to spin, sweeping them up. And, what is more, although they were off their faces by now, it seemed they could go on drinking, go on filling the glasses and lifting them to their lips. At least they still had that feeling, like a giant smile inside each one of them.

At four in the afternoon, just after the last of the builders had gone, Elisa came down to see what state her husband was in. She had to look around twice to find him, slumped as he was. She wasn't too alarmed, but she did check to see if there were any others left. And sure enough, the other two Chileans were there. As it happened, Pocketman emerged from a brief spell of unconsciousness and volunteered to help get her husband upstairs. She accepted: Raúl Viñas had come around sufficiently for the two of them to suffice. Almost restored to his normal lucidity by the climb, Pocketman offered to chain up the gate from the outside, although he wouldn't be able to lock it. After saying good-bye, he went back down. The remaining Chilean, Castro, was still sleeping, but when Pocketman gave him a shake, he woke up completely, if in a bad mood, and since they were both going in the same direction, and a fair way (they had to take the train), they headed off together, placidly, though not entirely steady on their legs. Pocketman kept his promise of chaining up the gate, so unless someone took the trouble of looking for the absent lock, the building appeared to be securely shut. It wasn't really, but there weren't any passersby. It was siesta time, the quietest and most deserted time of day, and the hottest. The silence was complete.

When the man of the house was peacefully unconscious in bed, covered only with a fine sweat of wine, Elisa asked Patri if she could do her a favor, a big favor (she stressed these last words with a certain irritation), and go fetch the children, who shouldn't have run off in the first place. Patri, who was a model of good manners and respect, repressed a "huh!" but couldn't quite stifle a sigh, which made her feel immediately ashamed, although it had been as faint as a breeze in the far heights of the sky. Elisa, who was deeply Chilean in this as in all other respects, could perceive the subtlest shades of an intention. So she added a comment, to compensate for the unfortunate tone of her request—or, at least, to unhinge it and let it swing loose beyond, where the real words are, which have no meaning or force to compel. It was amazing, she said, that even in this heat they still had the energy to run off. Playing excited them so much they just couldn't get enough. It was the equivalent of "living" for adults: you're not going to decide to die when night comes just because you've been living all day. Patri smiled. Also, they had been up early, said her mother; and lack of sleep, which makes adults slow and drowsy, makes kids restless. But they'd have to take a nap, or they'd be unbearable at night. Patri couldn't promise that she'd be able to get Juan Sebastián to go to bed, or even his buddy Blanca Isabel. The older boy hated the siesta. Elisa thought for a moment. She had, in fact, seen them when she was coming upstairs

with her husband. She regretted not having told them to
follow her. Each time they saw their father in that state,
they thought he was sick and about to die; she could have
exploited that momentary terror and shut them away in
the dark. With a bit of an effort, they could get to sleep. If
they ran off, it was hopeless. Luckily there was no danger of
them getting out into the street. For some reason, that danger didn't exist. There was the possibility of a fall, from any
of the floors, since the building was still a concrete frame,
with just a few internal walls in place, not all of them, by
any means. But neither mother nor daughter mentioned
that possibility; it didn't even enter into their private reflections. They had once said that an adult was just as likely to
fall as a child; there was no difference, because the planet's
gravitational force worked in the same way on both. It was
like asking which weighed more, a kilo of lead or a kilo of
feathers. And that's why they were vaguely but deeply re-
volted by the way the owners of the apartments took such
care not to let their children approach the edges when they
visited, like that morning. If that was how they felt, why
were they buying the apartments in the first place? Why
didn't they go and live in houses at ground level? "We're
different," they thought, "we're Chilean."

But there was an easier way to do it after all, said Elisa,
and that was to take away the toy cars. Without them, there
would be no reason to remain at large. If she knew her children, and she was sure she did, it was bound to work. It had
sometimes worked for her in the past. Patri said they would

hide them. Her mother bent down calmly (they were at the door of the little apartment, talking in hushed voices, unnecessarily, since Viñas was sound asleep), and picked up the cardboard box full of toys. With an expert hand, she began to rummage through it. She knew every one of her children's toys. "The big yellow one, the red one, the little blue truck . . ." She calculated that exactly four were currently in their possession. She even told Patri which ones. But Patri wasn't paying much attention. She didn't think it would be possible to recover all the cars, and so bring in the children. As long as they still had one, just one, Juan Sebastián would stay awake all through the siesta, the little devil.

She went downstairs to the sixth floor. The quickest way to do it was to check the floors one by one, room by room. If they heard her, they would try to hide. She set about it systematically, but it was hard to concentrate because the heat and the time of day had dazed her. The sixth floor seemed endless. Her chances of finding anything in that void perpetually full of air were minimal, given the terrible brightness, which she had grown so used to, living up there as summer set in, that her pupils had shrunk permanently to pin-points. She didn't understand the arrangement of the rooms, which wasn't clear at that stage of the construction; but she felt there were too many of them. The trend toward having more and more rooms was, she felt, absurd. A family couldn't observe the protocol of a royal court. If people started multiplying rooms by their needs, they could float away into the infinite and never touch the ground of reality again. One for sewing, another for embroidery; one for eating, one for drinking, one for each activity, in short. The same room reproduced over and over, each one fulfilling some silly requirement, as if in a perpetually receding mirror. Her mother had put it very well, except that she hadn't gone far enough in her generalization. Because the illusion of exhaustivity affected things as well as people. In any case, the children weren't there.

When she went down to the fifth floor, she was already tired and her eyelids felt heavy, which surprised her slightly, since she didn't like the siesta—she was still a child in that respect. Having washed the lunch dishes and left the miniscule rooftop apartment impeccably clean and tidy (in so far as they could, given that it was still under construction), she and her mother had watched television. She would have liked to go on watching, but the time slot for the kind of show they preferred had come to an end, and the ones that were starting required a different kind of attention.

It might seem odd that at lunchtime, when Abel Reyes came up, his cousin Patri had greeted him with a kiss. A kiss on the cheek was a normal enough greeting; what might seem odd is that they needed to greet one another, when he had been working in the building since early that morning. But, as it happened, they hadn't seen each other, which was not unusual, because she hardly ever went down. Her mother did the shopping, and rarely needed help. Patri went down once a day, if that. She helped a lot around the apartment, watched television, and looked after her half-brothers and -sisters. She was pretty much a homebody, like all Chileans, except when they are tireless travelers (she was a bit of both). She was fifteen; her surname was Vicuña, like her mother's, because she had been born when her mother was single. Very quiet, very serious, pretty hands.

They weren't on the fifth floor either, as she was able to verify (or so she thought), by checking from the front to the back, room by room. The children weren't there, but the other characters, those bothersome ghosts, were legion. They were always around at that time. To see them, you just had to go and look. Although they kept their distance, with an air of unaccountable haughtiness. For some mysterious reason, they had started shouting, bursting into thunderous peals of laughter that shook the sky. Patri wouldn't have paid them any more attention than usual, if not for two rather particular circumstances. The first was that there weren't just two or three or four ghosts, as one might have expected, given their characteristic and constitutive rarity, but a veritable multitude, appearing here and there, then moving away, laughing and shouting all the while like exploding balloons. The second circumstance was even more remarkable: they were looking at her. Normally they didn't look; they didn't seem to pay attention to anything in particular, or even to have attention. They were like that now too, except that they seemed to be making an exception for her, as if she were the object of their ostentatious, senseless amusement. She didn't take offence, because it wasn't serious. It was more like a flying puppet show, an out-of-place, unseemly

kind of theater. She had seen naked men before, of course
(although not many); she didn't find that especially frightening. But there was something implausible about it, since
you wouldn't normally see men without clothes except in
particular situations. The way they were floating in the air
accentuated the ambivalent impression. She had occasionally heard them speak, and wondered about it afterward, for
a while. It seemed easy enough to take them by surprise, to
slip past behind them. But perhaps it wasn't so easy.

She leant out over the front balcony and looked down
at the empty street. A car whizzed past. She went through
the apartment, searching for the children, until she reached
the back, and looked down from there as well. The sun
was beating in; it was an oven. She thought she saw a body
falling, even faster than they normally do, the naked body
of a ghost, covered with fine, white dust. It might have
been an optical illusion, but she knew it wasn't when she
heard another volley of guffaws, a great choral outburst of
laughter so loud it was almost desperate. When she turned
back toward the stairs, they were there again, or had just appeared, some swinging back and forth stupidly, like garlands,
others perfectly balanced—they all were, in fact, it was just
that they were using different methods. A quick movement
behind her and a touch that felt particularly real made her
swing around suddenly. It was Blanca Isabel, looking at her
with a fading surprise. She was a pretty girl, an exception
in the family, lively, and very intelligent according to her
parents. Although she was startled and must have guessed

why her sister had come downstairs, a smile was hovering around her lips: she thought she had caught Patri peeking at a forbidden sight. She looked as if she were about to start humming. Patri didn't feel that she had been "peeking" at the ghost's genitalia, not at all. Their laughter proved her innocence. "Now we're going to take a nap," Patri said energetically, although she too was disconcerted. It was a bad tactic, because Blanca Isabel didn't feel like a nap, and ran away. She reached the stairs before Patri, and started going down, whispering something to the others, who must have been nearby. Patri knew she had to hurry if she wanted to catch them, but she was half-hearted about it. It was too hot, and she was tired. So she listened, helplessly, as they scattered. Nevertheless her momentum carried her to the stairwell. Juan Sebastián was looking up at her from the next landing, ready to go down to the third floor. "Let's go," she said, "or Mom will come and get you." "Why?" he replied. Children always ask why. "Because you have to take a nap." "I don't know how. How do you do it?" "Where are the others?" "How should I know?" Patri started going down and the boy took off. He was already down on the next floor. She'd be able to corner him eventually, if he went all the way down. But the rascal knew hiding places with two escape routes, so the chase could go on forever. It was no good. She raised her voice again hoping to scare him into submission. She was irritated and couldn't understand why he had to run away. She wasn't going any further. What a stupid, childish thing to be doing, chasing kids around at siesta time! If they didn't want to sleep, why should they? It made no difference to her, or to their health, why would it? But since she had come down to the fourth floor, she could fetch the baby girl, at least.

Luckily for her, little Ernesto was there, looking at her with his beautiful big, dark eyes. Hi, he said, as if hiding something. There was a wet patch on the wall, at a height that indicated clearly what had happened. The children were forbidden to urinate anywhere inside the building, but they did it anyway. She shook her head disapprovingly. I took out my weenie and did it, said the boy. I know how it works, but your dad's going to tell you off. My dad did it too. Here? she asked him. He looked around, mildly perplexed. He seemed to mean two things: first, "all the floors look the same to me" and, second, "they all take out their weenies." He was letting his thoughts show in that gentle, docile way because sleepiness was overcoming him irresistibly. And both aspects of his excuse were reasonable, in a way. The mood of summery exhibitionism prevailing on the site, accentuated perhaps by the imperfect, deceptive repetition from one floor to the next, didn't shock Patri (even she wasn't that naïve) so much as intrigue her. She'd seen the gangs of ghosts shaking their sturdy members and aiming the jets of urine at the sky, showering it over the first-floor patio (their favorite place for this sport) until rainbows with a metallic sheen appeared in the siesta's white glare. The day the big satellite dish was installed on the terrace, they spent hours doing it, perched on the edge.

You get to bed, or Mom's going to smack you, she said. Compliantly, half-asleep, Ernesto headed for the stairs. Where's Jacqueline, she asked? The two youngest children were never far apart. He shrugged his shoulders. Patri called her. I'm going, she said finally. She followed the little boy up the stairs. When she was half way up, Blanca Isabel appeared behind her, with the baby girl in her arms, intending to move her to a safe place on the third floor. Patri turned around and started back down. The movement was enough to make Blanca Isabel deposit her sister and take off alone, jumping down the stairs three at a time. Jacqueline burst into tears. As soon as Patri picked her up, she calmed down. She put her arms around Patri's neck and rested her head on her shoulder. She weighed nothing at all. Amazingly, she was still the size of a doll at the age of two. But, in fact, it was like that with all children. They might be relatively big or small for their age, but, compared to an adult, they were always tiny. They were human in every way, but on another scale. And that alone could render them unrecognizable, or give the impression that they had been produced by the baffling distortions of a dream. As Ernesto had said a moment ago: the weenie. That must be why children were always playing with scaled-down models of things: cars, houses, people. A miniature theater, with its doors opening and closing, over and over again. The previous night, on television, they had seen *The Kiss'n Cuddle Love Show*, in which two puppets, a frog and a bear recited the names of the birthday boys and girls, and those who had written in. They never missed the show, although they had never written in themselves. Anyway, the puppets appeared on a tiny scene, with two window shutters instead of a curtain, which opened when their act began, and closed again at the end. In the course of normal distracted viewing, Patri had assumed that the shutters opened on their own, as they seemed to do, or were pushed from the inside, or something like that. But last night a problem with the lighting or the general clumsiness of the production had allowed her to see that the white shutters were opened by hands in white gloves, which were supposed to be invisible. The children didn't realize, but she did. Her mother noticed too, and although they said nothing, both she and Patri thought of the ghosts. They said nothing because it wasn't worth the effort of opening their mouths. But now, in retrospect, Patri felt that the incident had a sexual significance, or connotations at least.

She asked Ernesto what game they had been playing. We were pretending that the people who came this morning were our parents. She sighed in disapproval. Appalling! That must have been the older two children; they were always coming up with ideas like that, the little devils.

The third floor was the same, yet different; it wrapped the three of them in a fresh layer of silence. They say that silence increases with height, but Patri, who lived at altitude most of the time, wasn't so sure about that. Anyway, if it was true, and if there was a gradual increase, the difference between one floor and the next should have been perceptible, at least for someone with a sensitive enough ear, a musician, for example, listening in reverse, as it were. As she went from the fourth to the fifth floor, she felt the silence thicken, but that didn't prove anything, because the data of reality, as she had observed in the past, were produced by chance, or rather by an inextricable accumulation of chances. Also, since it's well known that sounds rise (which must be because "they're lighter than air," as the saying goes, or a lighter kind of air), you should hear more noise as you go up; it should be quiet on the ground. True, sounds fade progressively as they rise, because height is a kind of distance. But under normal circumstances, human beings are at or near ground level. If a man were placed at a great height, and he looked down, somewhere near halfway he would see two corresponding limits, floating like magnetized Cartesian divers: the limit of the sound as it passed into imperceptibility, and that of his own hearing range. But those divers . . . men floating in the air . . . she knew what *that* was about. And speaking of noise (and magnetism too, come to think of it), the most clamorous and disturbing noises she had heard in her months on the site had been made by cats. The neighborhood was populated by strays. Their survival and proliferation were favored by the gardens of the Theological University, the car bodies that the police left permanently parked all along in front of the station, the square a hundred yards away, the convent school's enormous park (the size of a whole block) with its luxuriant foliage, and, above all, the empty buildings, each with its clientele of old witches who came twice a day to put out milk and hamburger steak. The way the cats howled was beyond belief. At first she had thought they were children gone crazy. But that wouldn't have been so bad. The inhumanity of the cats' screams gave them something extra. And their speed, because those sounds were produced in the course of races and escapes, as opposed to the karateka's shout, which issues from a still body. (Patri had taken karate lessons in Chile, on the advice of her stepfather. For various reasons, including her innate distaste for perfection, she had neglected to sit the exam which would have given her a blue belt. Even though blue was her favorite color.) The astonishing activity of the cats, obscene as it was, reminded her of the ghosts, who manifested themselves as the opposite of obscenity, as a kind of innocence.

In fact, they were manifesting themselves at that very moment. They were emerging from the light, from transparency: they were opaque, definitely opaque, but because of the whiteness of the cement dust, they were hard to distinguish from the light. Where could their covering have come from? It was true that everything was dusty on the building site, but the strange thing about the ghosts was how evenly covered they were with that white dust, every square inch of them. And there was quite a lot to cover because they were tall like Argentineans, and solidly built, even chubby. Although well proportioned in general, some of them, the majority in fact, had big bellies. Even their lips were powdered; even the soles of their feet! Only at odd moments, from certain points of view, could you see the foreskin at the tips of their penises parting to reveal a tiny circle of bright red, moist skin. It was the only touch of color on their bodies. Even birds fluttering around in ashes don't achieve such a uniform result. Patri traversed the air through which they had flowed, unworried by the thought of her breath mixing with theirs. She was walking on the ground. What a destiny: unwittingly, unwillingly thrust into the midst of a nudist colony.

Tired and annoyed, she paid them no attention. She was sleepy too; since she was barely out of childhood herself, she still needed quite a lot of sleep. She felt she had wasted time, but, on the other hand, it was time that was good for nothing except being wasted. That was in the nature of siesta-time. The mysterious men were watching her from a certain distance, but she couldn't really be bothered returning their gaze. The laughter, at least, had dissipated. There was something aloof and severe about those insubstantial gangs. They were simply there.

Elisa was waiting for them at the top of the stairs. What about the others? was the first thing she asked. Ernesto started to explain, but Patri shrugged her shoulders. I couldn't catch them, she said. They got away. Mother and daughter were silently resigned. Elisa took the children inside. It's so hot! said the boy, yielding to the truth. She put them in the bedroom, where their father was snoring. She didn't even wash their feet; in a few seconds they were perfectly quiet. In the dining room, Patri saw the bags left out, and remembered that there was shopping to do. When Elisa came out of the bedroom, she offered to go and do it, with a list. No, said her mother, I have to do it myself this time, because I still haven't worked out exactly what I'm going to buy; it'll depend what's there. No one made a fuss about meals in that family, as long as they were nutritious and tasty. On the way, Elisa added, I'll look for the other two and take them along. That was a good idea. But then she said: Since they're not going to sleep, I'll take them for ice cream. Patri frowned as if to say: Well that's a great way to punish them for misbehaving. *She* didn't get any ice cream, even though she loved it. You lie down too, said her mother. I guess that's what I'll be doing, she replied. Elisa put on her shoes and picked up the bags. Back in a bit. See you, said Patri.

Off she went. Patri removed the crochet rug with which she covered the sofa that was her bed. She pushed the chairs up against the table. She took off her dress and got under the sheet. It was uncomfortable, because of the heat, but it was the prudent thing to do, because that room was the entrance to the little apartment, and anyone could have come along. It was boiling hot. The silence had deepened and was almost complete, with a just a vague echo of cackling, which made her even sleepier. She shut her eyes straight away. And fell asleep.

She dreamed of the building on top of which she was sleeping, not as it would be later on, not seeing it finished and inhabited, but as it was now, that is, under construction. It was a calm vision, devoid of troubling portents or inventions, almost a verification of the facts. But there is always a difference between dreams and reality, which becomes clearer as the superficial contrast diminishes. The difference in this case was reflected in the architecture, which is, in itself, a reciprocal mirroring of what has already been built and what will be built eventually. The all-important bridge between the two reflections was provided by a third term: the unbuilt.

The unbuilt is characteristic of those arts whose realization requires the remunerated work of many people, the purchase of materials, the use of expensive equipment, etc. Cinema is the paradigmatic case: anyone can have an idea for a film, but then you need expertise, finance, personnel, and these obstacles mean that ninety-nine times out of a hundred the film doesn't get made. Which might make you wonder if the prodigious bother of it all—which technological advances have exacerbated if anything—isn't actually an essential part of cinema's charm, since, paradoxically, it gives everyone access to movie-making, in the form of pure daydreaming. It's the same in the other arts, to a greater or lesser extent. And yet it is possible to imagine an art in which the limitations of reality would be minimized, in which the made and the unmade would be indistinct, an art that would be instantaneously real, without ghosts. And perhaps that art exists, under the name of literature.

In this sense all the arts have a literary basis, built into their history and their myths. Architecture is no exception. In advanced, or at least sedentary, civilizations, building requires the collaboration of various kinds of tradesmen: bricklayers, carpenters, painters, then electricians, plumbers, glaziers, and so on. In nomadic cultures, dwellings are made by a single person, almost always a woman. Architecture is still symbolic, of course, but its social significations are manifest in the arrangement of dwellings within the camp. The same thing happens in literature: in the composition of some works, the author becomes a whole society, by means of a kind of symbolic condensation, writing with the real or virtual collaboration of all the culture's specialists, while others works are made by an individual, working alone like the nomadic woman, in which case society is signified by the arrangement of the writer's books in relation to the books of others, their periodic appearance, and so on.

But in Patri's dream the architectural analogy was developed a little further. In Africa there is a curious race of pygmies, the Mbutu, nomadic hunters without a chief or social hierarchies. They look after themselves, and everybody else, without dramas. Their communities are relatively small: twenty or thirty families. When they decide to set up camp, they choose a clearing in the jungle and the dwellings are arranged in a "ring," which, according to the anthropologists, is typical of egalitarian societies. The huts form a circle with an empty center. But anthropologists are dreamers too, sometimes. How could this ring be visible except from a plane? Needless to say, the Mbutu pygmies don't fly; if they were meant to fly, they would have been born with wings. Also it's debatable whether or not the center is empty, since it's occupied by the space that makes it a center. "Whoever speaks in the center is heard by all," say the anthropologists, alluding involuntarily to dream ventriloquism. The huts are isotopic shells, in which an opening can be made anywhere. The Mbutu make just one: a door, facing the neighbors they like best. Say the lady of the house is cross with her neighbor for some reason or other. No problem; they block up the door and open another one, facing the neighbors on the other side. The researchers who have observed this system fail to draw the logical conclusion: the house of a truly sociable Mbutu would be all doors, and so not a house at all; conversely, a finished and complete construction presupposes hostility.

A contrasting example: the Bushmen. They too are nomadic and their camps are arranged in a "ring". Except that there is something in the middle of their ring. They place their little houses around a tree; under the tree the chief of the group builds his hut; at the door of the hut the chief lights a fire. What was lacking from the Mbutu camp was not a center, but its symbol. Providing a symbol engages a process of symbolic accumulation: the tree, the chief, the fire . . . Why not a rose, a stuffed giraffe, a sunken boat, a mosquito that happened to alight on the earlobe of a Nazi spy, a downpour, or a replica of the Victory of Samothrace?

The little Bushmen are comical, but it's the same with the extremely serious Zulu, who are formidable hunters and warriors. Those who have had the misfortune of facing them in battle (for example, the son of the Emperor Napoleon III and Eugenia de Montijo) can confirm that they form a semi-circle, "enveloping" the enemy troops before annihilating them. This is a reproduction of the method they use for hunting. And their camps are arranged in the same way: a semi-circle of huts. When the method is transposed from hunting to war, there is a transition from the real to the symbolic, without any loss of practical efficacy. It's not that one level replaces the other; the levels can co-exist, and a Zulu might even try hunting a tasty zebra with a technique tried and tested on the imperial prince. The architecture of the camp, whatever its degree of realization (interpretations and intentions must be taken into account as well as actual huts), constitutes a return to the real, because life is real, and the Zulu have to live, as well as hunting and making war. But they return involuntarily, as it were, without any plan, the way dreams unfold. The centre of the village is a void elegantly furnished with a bloody suction.

The architectural key to the built / unbuilt opposition, which analogies fail to capture, is the flight of time toward space. And dreaming is that flight. (So it wasn't a pure co-incidence that Patri's dream was about architecture). Except in fables, people sleep in houses. Even if the houses haven't yet been built. And therein, perhaps, lies the origin, the original cell, of the sedentary life. While habits, whether sedentary or nomadic, are made of time, dreams are time-free. Dreams are pure space, the species arrayed in eternity. That exclusivity is what makes architecture an art. Beyond this point, the timeless mental material of the unbuilt is detached from the field of possibility, ceases to be the personal failure of an architect whose more daring projects stalled for want of financial backing, and becomes absolute. Even the mixture of the built and the unbuilt becomes absolute. The construction at whose summit Patri was sleeping was a real model of that mixture, by virtue of its incomplete state and everything the decorators were still planning to do. It was a step away from the absolute, waiting only for bricks, mortar and metal to expel time from its atomic matrix in a fluid maneuver. That was the purpose of the girl's dream.

Now if the unbuilt, or the mixture in which it participates, can be considered as a "mental" phenomenon, like dreaming or the general play of intentions, the mind, in turn, can be seen to depend on the phenomenon of the unbuilt, of which architecture is the exemplary manifestation.

There are societies in which the unbuilt dominates almost entirely: for example, among the Australian Aborigines, those "provincial spinsters" in the words of Lévi-Strauss. Instead of building, the Australians concentrate on thinking and dreaming the landscape in which they live, until by multiplying their stories they transform it into a complete and significant "construction." The process is not as exotic as it seems. It happens every day in the western world: it's the same as the "mental city," Joyce's Dublin, for instance. Which leads one to wonder whether unbuilt architecture might not, in fact, be literature. In urbanized societies, city planning doubles architecture, robbing its symbolic function. If, in nomadic societies, the arrangement of the camp performed a function that was not performed by the construction of houses, that is, symbolizing society, in the planning of large contemporary cities, where the buildings require the convergence of skills and know-how from a great range of social sectors, urban planning repeats a function already satisfactorily performed, and ends up having no function of it own (or rather it symbolizes the policing of society). But perhaps it would be better to say that it leaves a "symbolic vacancy," an energy unemployed by any current necessity. The Nias come to mind with their twin deities, Lowalani, who represents positive forces, and his enemy, Latura Dano, god of the negative. According to the Nias, the world is layered, made up of nine superposed planes, on the highest of which resides Lowanlani, sleeping with his consort, a nameless goddess (let's call her Patri), who is a kind of mediator. The planning of the Nia villages "represents" this construction, horizontally of course, the high, for example, corresponding to the right-hand side, and the low to the left, or whatever. Now the condominiums, the skyscrapers that the Nias haven't built (negating the negation of the unbuilt, as it were), would represent symbolism itself. From which it could be deduced that for every building there is a corresponding non-building. On the same principle, the natives of Madagascar make pretty wooden models of multi-story houses, crammed with little people and animals, which are used as toys. If those models represent anything, it is "the children's house," another form of the unbuilt.

But the Australians, what do the Australians do? How do they structure their landscape? For a start they postulate a primal builder, whose work they presume only to interpret: the mythical animal who was active in the "dreamtime," that is, a primal era, beyond verification, as the name indicates. A time of sleep. The visible landscape is an effect of causes that are to be found in the dreamtime. For example the snake that dragged itself over this plain creating these undulations, etc., etc. These "intellectual dandies," these "spinsters," these curious Aborigines make sure their eyes are closed while events take place, which allows them to see places as records of events. But what they see is a kind of dream, and they wake into a reverie, since the real story (the snake, not the hills) happened while they were asleep.

The dreamtime, as giver of meaning or guarantor of the stability of meanings, is the equivalent of language. But why did the Australian Aborigines need an equivalent? Didn't they already have languages? Maybe they also wanted a hieroglyphic script, like the Egyptians, and they made it from the ground under their feet.

The elements of Australian geography are as simple as they are effective: the point and the line, that's it. As the Aborigines proceed over plains and through forests, the point and the line are represented by the halt and the journey. With a line and a point, a line that passes through many points in the course of a year, frequently changing direction, they trace out a vast drawing, the representation of destiny. But there is something very special going on here:

via the point, the precise point in space, the nomads can pass through to the other side, like a dressmaker's pin or needle, through to the side of dreaming, which changes the nature of the line: the hunting or gathering route becomes a mythic itinerary. Which adds a third dimension to the drawing of destiny. But the passage through the point is happening all the time, since no point is specially privileged (not even waterholes—contrary to the anthropologists' initial assumptions—although they serve as models for the points of passage, which can, by rights, be found anywhere, at any point along the line), so the food-gathering route is always taking on a mythical significance and vice versa. There is something dreamlike about the points that provide a view of the other side, but they belong not so much to the dreamtime as to dream work. The nomads enter the dreamtime not by setting off on some extraordinary, dangerous voyage, but through their everyday, ambulatory movement.

To symbolize the point, the Australian Aborigines have a "sacred post" (a rough translation, of course, because it's not sacred in the western sense), which they carry with them and drive into the ground when they camp each night, at a slight angle, like the tower of Pisa, to indicate the direction they will take the next day. This post is decorated with carvings, which allude to the mythic itinerary, and in this way it combines the two contrasting motifs of the halt (signaled by the place where the post has been driven into the ground) and the itinerary (doubly represented by its inclination and the carvings, since the itinerary has two aspects, relating to food-gathering and to myth, while the point is single in its nature—it is always a point of passage.)

But Patri's dream went further, higher, taking in different systems, which were increasingly original and strange. In some cases the construction of the landscape, common to a great variety of carefree indigenous peoples, was simplified to the extreme. For example by certain Polynesian islanders, whose landscape consists entirely of those specks of earth or coral emerging from the sea, which seem to be adrift . . . They have a simple fix for this, using two lines that are not so much imaginary as utilitarian: one from the island down to the bottom of the sea, like an anchor, the other up to a star at the zenith, to stop the island from sinking.

And even the Polynesian system is complicated compared to some others, especially virtual systems, which start from humanity and proceed toward thought—an itinerary which, in turn, is doubled with dreaming.

After non-building comes its logical antecedent, building. As a real practice, building is decoration. In architecture, decoration is always an expansion, expanding anything and everything, until only the process of expansion remains. In agricultural societies, the accumulation of goods and the management of social inequalities gives building the function of creating an "artificial world," in which the privileged are confined by their status, whatever it may be (even the status of pariah). At which point architecture (paradoxically) becomes "real"; and if, until then, the world—the landscape or the territory—had been humanity's artistic miniature, its little dream-lantern, now the opposite phase begins, the phase of expansion, which gives rise to decoration, which is everything.

The development of "real" architecture, that is, of the decorative elements, is directly linked to the possibility of accumulating provisions for the workers or the slaves who do the building, and don't have time to go hunting or gathering food. Such accumulations result in inequalities. There is a mechanism for reducing excessive accumulation, and regulating wealth (without regulation there would be no wealth): *potlatch*, the festivity that involves squandering food and drink and other sorts of goods in a brief, crazy splurge, and so reducing the stocks to a satisfactory level. By staging a grand and brilliant spectacle, comparable to a temporary or perishable work of art, the festivity performs the function of attracting the greatest possible quantity of people. The size of the audience on the day is crucial, since this artistic manifestation will not endure in time. Art, in all its forms, has an inherent economy, and this case is no exception.

The *potlatch*, of course, belongs to the prehistory, or the genealogy, of festivities and partying, because with the passage of time, an alternative must arise at some point: instead of more and more people being present, a subtler form of sociability limits attendance to special people, the people that matter. The logical conclusion of this process is the single-person party, and the best model for that is dreaming.

In Patri's dream the building on the Calle José Bonifacio was under construction. Standing still yet seized by an
interior, interstitial movement. Suddenly a wind, a typical
dream-wind, so typical that dreams might be said to consist
of it, arose and blew the building apart, reducing it to little
cubes the size of dice. This was the transition to the world
of cartoons. The building was reconstructed somewhere
else, in another form, its atoms recombined. Then it disinte-
grated again, the wind scattering its particles, one of which
came to rest on Patri's open eye, and in its microscopic
interior, an entire house was visible, with all its rooms and
furniture, its candelabras, carpets, glassware, and the little
golden mill that spins in the wind from the stars.

Two hours after going down, Elisa Vicuña came back up
the stairs, laden with bags full of shopping. The heat had not
eased off in the least; on the contrary. It was the time of day
when one suspects the climate of malevolence. She climbed
the last flights of stairs on her own, because Juan Sebastián and Blanca Isabel went to get the toy cars they had
left behind and resumed their games; not that they really
wanted to go on playing, but they were still scared that
their mother would put them to bed. There was no danger
of that any more, because the hour of the siesta had passed,
but just in case, and out of sheer willfulness, they ran away.
They had been to an ice-cream shop with air conditioning,
where they had stayed a fair while. The cool interlude had
refreshed them a bit, but the contrast when they came out
made the persistence of the heat all the more terrible. Elisa

saw that her eldest daughter was asleep. She didn't wake her up. She went to the kitchen, and took the shopping out of the bags, but didn't put anything in the fridge, because they didn't have a fridge. Then she started washing. They didn't have a washing machine either, but that didn't bother her too much, although she would have liked one. In fact she enjoyed washing, and spent quite a lot on soaps and special products, as well as the bleach. Oddly, for someone who was so fond of this pastime, her hands were not ruined. So what if those two brats didn't want to sleep. She hadn't taken a siesta today either; she didn't feel like it. For various reasons, the washing had built up. She filled the two washbowls and the two plastic buckets, and began to make a mixture of various products, which she always finished off with a healthy squirt of bleach. She started scrubbing some of the kids' little T-shirts. She felt depressed, because of the heat, because of all the work she had done already that day, and what remained to do, because of the end of the year, and her husband, and so on, and so on. It wasn't a momentary low. She was going through a period of depression due mainly to the fact that they hadn't moved, as she had hoped, or rather planned. Her husband had been tempted by the special bonus they had promised him if he stayed until the building was finished. By now, she thought, she should have been in the new place. Not that it was better, but she had got used to the idea, and no one likes having to give up an idea, even, or especially, if it doesn't have have any intrinsic merit. She would buy something with the extra money, but it wouldn't be the same: money and new things, they were explicable, whereas her idea of moving before the end of the year was beyond explanation; it belonged to the world of whim. Anyway, it was Raúl's decision, and today he would get to hit the booze twice. He often scored a double: lunch and dinner. What a liver he must have! thought his wife. It's incredible, it must be made of iron. Drunks were tougher all round, or in a different way from normal people; she liked the feeling of being protected by that superhuman vigor. What other protection did she have? She liked a lot of things about her husband and had no desire to complain about him, not even in the privacy of her ruminations. For example, she couldn't imagine herself married to a sober man.

As she put some of Patri's clothes into the wash, Elisa's thoughts turned to her daughter: now *she* was a more serious worry. Elisa had never known such a mixed-up girl. No one could say how she would turn out, least of all her mother. It was partly her age of course, but even so, she was a particularly worrying case. She never stuck at anything; she had no perseverance, as if she didn't really know what she liked. If only she would fall in love! Proceeding mechanically through the washing, Elisa set out the problem point by point. Like many Chileans, she had the secret and inoffensive habit of addressing long, casuistic explanations to an imaginary interlocutor, or rather a real but physically absent person. In her case it was a friend she hadn't seen for years, not since she had come to Buenos Aires, even longer, in fact. Nevertheless, it was to this friend that she explained the case of her eldest daughter. Look, she didn't even stick with the karate; that was my husband's bright idea, typical! But at least it was something. And those mother-of-pearl buttons she used to polish so nicely, she gave that up too, even sooner. I can't really blame her for that, though, because we moved here. OK. But what about school? Same again: she refused to sit the equivalence tests. She wanted to be an electrician. Crazy! *I'd* have as much hope of doing that. As Elisa explained to her absent friend, the fundamental problem and the source of all the others, was Patri's frivolity. Was there ever a more frivolous girl in the world? It was hard to imagine. She didn't take serious things seriously because she was always serious about something else. She was a little dreamer, living in a looking-glass world. Not that she wasn't intelligent; but her frivolity made her come across as silly. She had talent, and plenty of it. She was a talented seamstress, for a start. She could have been earning a living already from her sewing, if she'd wanted to. There was some hope, then, for the future, faint though it was, because sewing was a frivolous occupation. All that mattered was the result, not the intentions, which could be supremely whimsical. And Patri's whims were limitless. For example, six years ago, when Blanca Isabel was born, she had prevailed against Elisa and insisted on choosing the baby's name. It was the name of a famous fashion designer: an Argentinean woman, but the daughter of a Chilean, who in turn was the daughter of a woman who had been the godmother of Raúl Viñas's grandfather. Elisa's heart had been set on baptizing the child Maruxa Jacqueline, a desire she had partially satisfied later on, with her youngest girl.

Her soliloquy was interrupted by a feeling she often had, the semi-epileptic impression that someone was passing behind her. There was no one behind her in the kitchen, and no room anyway, but through the open door she could see a band of ten ghosts watching her from the terrace, between the apartment and the stairs. What were those floury clowns doing there, she wondered crossly. She didn't like it when they interrupted her conversations with an intimate friend, all the more intimate for being in her mind and nowhere else. (Elisa didn't know it, but a few months earlier, a horrific derailment in Concepción had claimed her friend's life.) Anyway, it wasn't their normal time. Were they going to start showing up around the clock? Or was there something special happening because it was the last day of the year? That could have explained why they were staring at her with their round eyes open wide in their stupid faces. As if they had something to propose to her. It was odd, because they were meant to be seen rather than to see. And since she was in the relatively dark interior of the kitchen, she may not have been visible from outside. But she couldn't be sure about that, because even if the shadows hid everything else, her thick, twelve-diopter spectacles could reflect or condense enough light to make them visible (she had been caught out like that before): two shining circles, like the eyes of an owl suspended in the night. In any case, she could see *them*, and that must have been their way of watching. But was she really seeing them, or was it a waking dream? Ah, that was another question. Seeing ten naked men with their dicks dangling while washing clothes in the kitchen wasn't exactly the most realistic experience. Although for a married woman like her, the scene had a special significance, not a promise but a confirmation: men were all the same in the end. They had nothing to hide. It wasn't just that all men had the same bits; they also had the same value. Which was, admittedly, considerable, but it was shared out among a multitude that was almost beyond the grasp of the imagination, like the idea of "everyone." The only thing that bothered her was the bad influence the ghosts might have on her children, particularly on her frivolous elder daughter. Since Patri was given to building castles in the air, certain chimerical spectacles could lead her to the utterly misguided belief that reality is everywhere. It was just as well that the family would soon be leaving the building site. They would have left already, if her husband had listened to her. Meanwhile those jerks were still staring at her. Or was it the other way round? She turned away and went on with the washing, trying to concentrate; what with the distraction she'd probably gone and put in too much bleach. She was always doing that.

She was nearly finished when the apparition of Patri at her side gave her a start. Heavens, I didn't see you come in, she said, to hide her agitation. A little sleep and look at me, said Patri, displaying her arms, shoulders and neck, covered with sweat. They spent a moment complaining about the heat. Hey, I'd like to have a shower, said Patri, if that's OK with you. Of course, said her mother; I'm just about finished anyway, see. Just wait till I rinse this out . . . there . . . just the sight of that cold water running . . . I'll have a shower, too, after . . . and this one . . . there we go. She turned off the faucet. All yours; careful not to wake the kids. They had to take all these precautions because when water was coming out of one faucet, it wouldn't come out of another, and if they turned on two at once it didn't come out of either. It was something they had discovered simply by living there. No doubt some problem with the plumbing, or rather with the general design of the building, which would have disastrous consequences for its occupants later on. Raúl Viñas felt it was best not to tell the architect. Why did he need to know? So he could get uptight about it? The Chilean builder regarded the problem as insoluble, so what was the point? As for them, they managed all right, turning off one faucet before they opened another, politely asking permission. It wouldn't be so simple when the apartments were occupied, but they would be gone by then. Patri went to the bathroom and turned on the shower. Elisa heard the beatific murmur of the water. She took the buckets full of rinsed and wrung-out washing and went out to where she had strung up a line on the terrace, in front of the big frame for the games room and the pool. The sun's force was brutal, even though it had begun to go down. The clothes would be dry in a flash, she thought. Pity there wasn't the slightest breeze. The ghosts were still hanging around. They had scattered now, but there were more of them. Some were sitting on the sharp edges of the parabolic dish, as they liked to do; it was a bit of a shock to see them there, but of course they didn't feel the sharp edge. And even to say they were sitting was a fiction as Elisa could tell by the way they were "seated" all around the edge, even on the bottom, that is, upside down. Perhaps because there was something different about them at that hour of the day, she was vaguely troubled, for the first time, by a serious concern: they were *like* men, and you couldn't help seeing them as such; but there was also the possibility of seeing them as *real* men, while knowing they were images. As she hung out the washing, it struck her that with so many men available, the key was to choose the right one. But how? She discussed it with her imaginary friend. It's not that there's a shortage of men, she said, with a chuckle that was imaginary too, but they're never there when you need them. The sun was already making her feel faint and giving her a headache, so she finished hanging out the washing and went straight back inside without even glancing at those creatures, leaving the dining room door slightly ajar in the hope that some air would flow through. She went to the bedroom to have a look: Raúl Viñas was sleeping soundly, the two little one as well. She half-closed that door too, and switched on the television, with the sound down low. Patri came out of the bathroom with wet hair, fresh and smiling. Do you feel better now? Sure, see the difference? I could have spent hours under that shower. Well, when we fill up the pool, you can splash around in it all day long, huh? Has it started already? asked Patri. I don't know, I just put it on; OK, let's see, it's about to start, I think.

There was a soap opera that they watched at six. They loved the story, although, since they weren't completely stupid, they realized how bad it was. But that didn't really matter, as long as they didn't lose the thread, and, surprisingly, they never did. Women lived in a world of stories, according to Elisa, surrounded, smothered, submerged by fascinating stories. Mother and daughter had watched a good many soap operas over the years and could safely say that they were all the same, but they didn't regret having watched them. The plots always revolved around pregnancy and money. The link between the two themes was a woman who became wealthy, immensely wealthy, the better to scorn the man who had got her pregnant when she was poor. The charm lay in the incongruous balance between the superfluous and the important. With the benefit of her experience, Elisa could easily dismiss the questions of money as secondary and concentrate on the rest. Moving from the relative to the absolute, if only in fiction, made her happy. (For her daughter it was very different, although equally enjoyable.) Almost every evening at that time, they would sit down, just the two of them, in front of the television, to watch the story of young Esmeralda, who had risen from being a slave, held in secret on an anachronistic plantation in Costa Rica, to owning vast oilfields on the

Arabian peninsula. They discussed the issues as they arose
in the story. Elisa would try to point out certain things
to her daughter, who obstinately refused to see them, or
would only see them from her own point of view. It was a
little one-student school, in which practically nothing was
learned, although you never can tell. The question of pregnancy, for example, was more complex than it might have
seemed at first. Elisa had got pregnant with Patri when
she was as old as Patri was now. The father, so she said, was
the best man in the world. He had disappeared from her
life, like most childhood memories. That was the problem
with men: they weren't definitive, they weren't right. But
Mom, objected Patri, I'm going to find the right man in
the end, like Esmeralda, I hope. In the end, yes, in the
end, said Elisa emphatically, in the end . . . maybe. But not
before. And when you think about it, what's a pregnancy?
She pointed to the screen: Do you suppose that actress was
really pregnant when all this was happening in the story?
Of course not. You have to be very careful not to mix up
truth and lies, reality and fiction. Yeah, but you really got
pregnant, didn't you? Or were you just an image, a hypoth-
esis? Elisa laughed. It was true, in a way; that was what she
had been. Amazingly her adolescent daughter had touched
on a very deep truth, and yet, at the same time—there's
always another side to things—it was a truth composed of
silences and suppositions. For example, she had never confessed the identity of "the best man in the world" to her
parents. They had made an incorrect supposition. In fact,

she thought, during a commercial break between chapters of the soap opera, she had made an incorrect supposition herself. Because later, a few years later, Raúl Viñas had appeared in her life, and everything had changed.

There you go, said Patri, as if she had hit on the most convincing argument: Isn't he the right one? Her mother replied with a smile. All her friends and acquaintances knew what a loving couple Elisa and her husband were, a real example. For just that reason, there was something elusive about their love. If her daughter found that disconcerting, well, she was sorry, but there was nothing she could do. Some things took time to understand. And Elisa was as quick as anyone to recognize her husband's faults, such as his fondness for drink. It was no more justifiable than any other vice, but Elisa came up with good explanations for it. For example, that by drinking glass after glass of wine, in interminable sessions, Raúl Viñas was gathering momentum in his quest for the infinite. It was like swallowing the sea, as they say, and what was wrong with that? It might be terrible to have that kind of thirst, but for those who don't, it's a magnificent spectacle. And another thing: Raúl Viñas was one the few happy men left on earth, or at least in Chile, where they would have stayed if Elisa Vicuña's opinions had carried any weight. Happiness always brings happiness, and plenitude, in its wake.

But we're poor, look at how we live, Patri replied, pointing to the stifling, cramped, unfinished apartment. But that doesn't matter, girl, why should that matter? We're healthy aren't we, we have enough to eat, and beautiful children playing happily, and loving relatives and friends? You are *so optimistic*, said Patri, with the expression of someone confronting an utter impossibility. Her mother was laughing. Don't you see, girl. I've been lucky. It's not funny, Mom. But I'm not joking, sweetie. The thing is to find a real man, even if he has all the faults in the world. A real man. A real man. She repeated the phrase mechanically as their conversation languished—the story was beginning again. In all the splendor of her incredible beauty, the heroine signed the papers that would make her the legal owner of the Palace of Versailles, which the socialist government of France had sold to raise money for the development of advanced technology. This is so absurd, said Patri under her breath. Just like our lives, said her mother, who hadn't taken her eyes off the screen. A number of typical soap-opera clues had led them to suspect that the heroine's lover, a Japanese magnate whom she had supposed dead after a crash landing in the Azores, was about to reappear, and both of them knew that when he did, when he opened the door . . . they would cry.

It must have been around seven, the soap opera had finished on a note of suspense, relating, of course to Esmeralda's reproductive system (if she could be said to *have* one since, in a sense, she *was* an exquisite and luxurious reproductive system), and they had switched off the television, when they heard a din rising from below. Someone's coming, said Elisa, announcing only one of the possibilities, although it was rather early for the guests to start arriving. But as the old saying goes: "Evening's guests arrive by day." If they do, she remarked, they'll get a splendid reception, with half the family asleep. Within seconds she recognized the voices of the children, who didn't even give them time to get up from their chairs: Juan Sebastián came running in shouting: Look what Aunty Inés brought me, one for each of us, this one's mine, etc. etc. With urgent sign language Elisa implored him to lower the volume. It was as if the kid had a megaphone in his mouth. Can't you see the others are sleeping? Yeah, yeah, OK, he conceded impatiently; but they had to understand, he was thinking about the presents. He had already put four toy cars on the table; they were made of plastic and all the same, down to the color: red. Blanca Isabel came in like a whirlwind and pounced. This one's mine! They started shouting again, inevitably. The eldest child had of course taken the initiative of opening the packet. Each of them seized a car; although the cars were identical, there was an obvious advantage in being able to choose while the other two children were asleep. What a surprise they would get, poor suckers, when they found they could only choose between the two remaining toy cars, which where indistinguishable from the others! Juan Sebastián and Blanca Isabel reveled in their triumph. Elisa went to the door, which had been left wide open, and waited for her sister-in-law, who, influenced somehow by the soap opera's delaying tactics, or simply because the children had come rocketing up, seemed to take forever to appear. Elisa's curiosity was particularly piqued because her sister-in-law had arranged to come with her boyfriend, who still hadn't met the family. If he had come too, it was odd that she couldn't hear them talking. Or maybe they had stopped to look at the apartments? Maybe she had come early to help, and he'd be turning up later.

At last the extraordinary Inés Viñas made her appearance. Predictably, she had climbed the stairs at a leisurely pace and wasn't even out of breath. Are you on your own? said Elisa as soon as she saw her. Roberto's coming later, dear, I came early to give you a hand. But you didn't need to bother, etc. etc. They gave each other a kiss without interrupting their conversation. You couldn't find two more typical Chilean women. And seeing them together, it was striking the way they realized the type, almost to the point of caricature. The coincidence was especially notable because they were so physically different. Inés Viñas was quite short and petite. Her skin had a more olive tone; her hair was a shinier black, and her cheeks were sunken (while Elisa Vicuña's were round and somewhat childlike). She was quite pretty and rather flamboyant, within the demure limits imposed by her family and nationality. She was wearing stylish white sandals, an Indian skirt and a blue cotton tee shirt. And long earrings. You look really well. Not as well as you. No you do, really. Come off it, can't you tell I had a cough? What do you mean, a cough? Like I said, one of these days I'm going to catch pneumonia. She's so funny this girl, she kills me! Hi Patri! Patri was extraordinarily Chilean too. Seeing the three of them together made it even more noticeable. You washed your hair? See how awful mine is? Come on, mine's much worse. I told you to be quiet, you kids! The older children wanted to make off with the toy cars that belonged to the others. No, said Elisa Vicuña, You leave them there. Oh, poor things, said Inés Viñas, I'll wrap them up again. No, don't, this little devil ripped the paper. It was already ripped, shrieked the boy. Are they asleep? asked the guest lowering her voice, which, since she was Chilean, was already very soft. Your brother too, said Elisa. The three of them put on highly stylized laughing expressions. They found it seriously funny. Still napping at seven! All right, off you go, said Elisa. Silly of me, wasn't it. Four exactly the same. I didn't know what to get them. You shouldn't have bothered, dear. It wasn't much of a bother: the same thing for all four! Inés dear, it's perfect. Before I forget, I brought something for you too, Patricita. For me?! Listen, Elisa, Roberto is going to bring some bottles of wine . . . That's too kind! But you don't have to, you know, I'm not a little girl any more. Look, it's just something small. Patri removed the gift with great care from the little paper envelope: it was a bracelet of colored beads. Her pleasure and gratitude soared to indescribable heights. She put it on straight away, and it looked very nice on her. What a cute bracelet! They moved on to more general topics. How about this heat? said Inés Viñas. It doesn't let up, does it? asked and confirmed her sister-in-law. There must be a bit of breeze here, though. Don't you believe it. Isn't there? Well, yes, but only sometimes. That was understandable. What I can't understand, said Inés, is why you came to live in this birdcage. They laughed.

Meanwhile, the children had woken up. A bit of crying and moaning: here we go, said Elisa Vicuña. She went into the bedroom and came back with the two little monsters, one under each arm, naked and crying, covered with perspiration. Their aunt gave them a kiss, laughing at the way they were carrying on. She had an easy manner with children, which calmed them down, and even these little ones were alert to the word "present." The two toy cars had been wrapped up again, and the parcel was on the table. A little bath first, said Elisa. I'll give you a hand. No, don't worry, it won't take long … you'll see … I'll just give them a splash … She went into the bathroom and poured some water over the children, which woke them up properly. Patri, she called from the bathroom: Go and tell the others to come for their snack. Patri went out. Hey, is Javier coming? In a minute, said Elisa. With the whole family. The two children, with wet hair, were deposited on top of the table, and Ernesto began to open the parcel. Aunt Inés cuddled them. The little girl was so tiny and sweet. She's always smiling, isn't she! She's lovely! Elisa was preparing something in the kitchen. How can I help? asked her sister-in-law. I'm fine, in a minute I'll give you their shoes and you can put them on. Where are they? Hold on, said Elisa, heading for the bedroom, I'll get them for you now. As she took the children's shoes, Inés said: And that man is still asleep, is he? Uh huh, like a log, takes a fair bit to wake him up. The two older children came in. You haven't gone and broken the cars already, have you? said their mother. No, no! See! They displayed them, intact. Patri had come in quietly and was looking at the bracelet on her wrist. Inés Viñas finished putting on the children's shoes, and told them each to sit on a chair, with their red toy cars, if they liked (but the best thing, said Juan Sebastián, is crashing them), while their mother poured them each a big glass of milk. So you must have bought a fridge, said Inés, looking at the glasses . . . No, no. They're going to lend us one. This is special milk, it keeps without a fridge. Oh yes, I know, said Inés.

While the children were busy with their afternoon snack, Inés Viñas made the following remark: The last time I was here, not even ten days ago, you could see right through each floor, but today on the way up . . . Her sister-in-law interrupted: So you saw the partition walls? They've put most of them up already; they might even have finished. Hey, can we look at them? At what? At the apartments, dear. Sure, straight away! The owners won't come? Why would they come, at this time of day, on New Year's Eve? Anyway, Patri put in, they were all here this morning. Were they? Why? I don't know, said Elisa . . . I think there was a meeting. You wouldn't believe how many people there were. We stayed in here, while they came and went.

Then they told the children to finish their milk while they went down to look at the apartments. But they could have saved their breath: the four of them guzzled down what was left so they could come along. They began the

descent chatting brightly. They guessed at the layout of the
rooms from what they could see. The upper floors were
more finished. Patri was quite amazed by their suppositions,
which would never have occurred to her. She knew that
those rooms would be bedrooms, dining rooms, bathrooms,
or kitchens, but she had never wondered which would be
which. The other two were even doing imaginary swaps: I
wouldn't put the living room here; I'd make this my bedroom. Other aspects of the apartments made them laugh.
They'll have to put up huge drapes, said one, and the other
replied: Except they don't have neighbors looking in, that's
the advantage. They went down from the sixth floor to the
fifth, and from the fifth to the fourth, talking all the way.
They ranked the floors according to preference. Look at
the way these rich people live, said Inés Viñas. And they're
going to splash around up there too? Elisa looked up at the
ceiling, bewildered for a moment, until she remembered
the swimming pool. How do you like that, she remarked, a
pool on the rooftop terrace! I couldn't *believe* it, until I saw
it with my own eyes, or rather till I saw they were building
it. It's just incredible, said Inés. Isn't it? said Patri, who was
taking a very small part in the conversation. Some things
are unbelievable, said the visitor, but when you see them
with your own eyes, you have to bow to the evidence. Yes,
said Patri.

As they visited the apartments methodically, from one
end to the other, the question of evidence led to two topics that were, not unreasonably, dear to their hearts: medi-

cine and marriage. Inés Viñas swore by homeopathy and warmly recommended it at every opportunity. She saw her little old homeopath as a kind of shaman whose precise and parsimonious doses could cure anything. Her sister-in-law Elisa, while not a supporter of allopathy (it didn't deserve supporters, she admitted, since it was just a business) favored conventional medicine, because she had a problem with belief. There are people who just can't believe, she said, and I'm one of them. But you could make an effort! said Inés. If it was only a matter of making an effort, I would have done it already, if only to please you, replied Elisa. Well *don't* make an effort, then, just believe! Elisa: The thing is, you *have* to make an effort. And not believing is simply not being able to do that. Elisa dear, I really can't follow you, although I'm trying, I swear. Come on, what if you gave it a go? This whole conversation was abstract, in a manner of speaking, because neither of them was ill or thought she was. Which probably explains why they could reason about it. Look, Inés, homeopathy, or any other kind of magical medicine, only works for those who believe. That's where you're wrong, Elisa! Lots of people who didn't believe have been cured. Is that so? But didn't they believe afterward? Of course, why wouldn't they? That's what I mean: you have to believe, either before or after. But it's not the same thing! It doesn't matter: I'd only be convinced by someone who didn't believe at all, someone who had been cured, and went on not believing. But that's impossible! Exactly, you see what I mean?

While talking about medicine they were also talking about marriage. If there was any disagreement on that topic, it was subtler. Because all women, or nearly (all the ones they knew, anyway) got married, sooner or later. It was a kind of universal homeopathy, which sent belief leaping wildly, all over the place, with nothing to guide it. Patri, whose part in the conversation was limited to an odd monosyllable or chuckle, was listening carefully. Inés Viñas sensed this attention, and looked thoughtfully at the girl.

When they had seen enough of that layered, multi-family mansion, and there was nothing left to criticize in their good-natured, skeptical way, they started going back upstairs, without so much as a moment's pause in their chatter. Which, come to think of it, was, in itself, something to be marveled at, a challenge to belief: how is it that conversation topics keep coming up, one after another, inexhaustibly, as if they weren't tied to objects, which are finite, as if they were pure form? It went to show that life had hidden recesses. When they reached the top of the building, the heat, which had not eased off in spite of the late hour, reminded the hostess of something they still hadn't bought, because they were leaving it till the last minute: ice. She asked Patri if she would do her a favor and fetch it. Patri went to get the bag, and her mother told her to take some money from her purse. Patri was thinking: Where does all the money come from? We're always spending it, but there's always some left. Her mother had a reputation in the family as a good housekeeper. And she was in fact fairly good, but the reputation was based on a misunderstanding: seeing the whole family dressed in faded clothes, the relatives supposed that Elisa Vicuña was extremely thrifty and economical. To tell the truth, they couldn't understand how clothes that were so faded, almost white, and therefore, they supposed, very old (when in fact they might have been bought the week before) remained in one piece: it could only be explained by infinite care and vigilance. When Patri came back with the bag and the money, Inés Viñas, who was at the edge of the empty swimming pool, admiring that huge absurdity, offered to go with her. No, there's no need; it's not far, just round the corner. We'll get two bags then, to make the drinks extra cold, replied Inés, laughing. Don't worry, don't worry, said mother and daughter, but she insisted. Since she had come to bother them so early, she might as well help with something.

Inés and Patri went downstairs and out into the street, which was coming back to life. Inés asked if she had friends in the neighborhood. No, replied Patri, I hardly ever go down. This is the first time I've been down in two days. Inés was amazed. She couldn't imagine it. And how are you going to find a boyfriend like that, my girl? Patri laughed in reply, and Inés joined in.

Hey, don't laugh, I'm serious. Didn't you hear what we were saying, your mom and me? Yes, but I still don't know who I'm going to marry. Inés took a few steps in silence, wondering what to say. Never say you don't know. Why not? Because. Patri chose to respond with a chuckle. Tell me, said

Inés, You're not a virgin, are you? No, not any more. Uhuh, but weren't you worried about getting pregnant? This time it was Patri's turn to ponder her reply. Eventually she came out with: More or less. What a funny answer! said Inés and burst out laughing. But you're a funny girl all round, aren't you, Patricita! Hearing her laugh made Patri laugh too. They went into the store that sold ice, made their purchase, and, when they came out again, started talking about love. It's the most important thing, the only thing there is in the world. Yes, yes, of course, said Patri. Why do you say you don't know who you're going to marry? Because it's true. Even so ... They walked a while in silence. The trees in the street were as still as plaster statues. It's so hot, said the younger of the two. It's a heat wave, really, said the other, then added: You know what that means, don't you? There'll be a big, long storm afterward and then it'll be cold. Are you sure? It's hard to believe. That's how it is. That's what always happens in Buenos Aires. The weather does one thing, then the other. I think it does that everywhere, said Patri with a certain irony. Yes, but here, said Inés, it's more pronounced and it happens every time. What does? The downpour. Ah, said Patri, looking at the spotless blue sky. No, not now, but you'll see. Changing the subject abruptly, Inés remarked: There are some really good-looking men. Yes, there are some I find very attractive. There are some I find *extremely* attractive. Well, me too, if we're going to extremes. But, you know, they can turn out to be bastards. Yeah, of course; that's always happening on TV. But that's fake. Didn't you just say . . . ? No, what I'm saying is they *can* be bastards. Like they can be anything, Inés added. Oh, OK, all right. But the really important thing, in love, is to find a real man. Not the real men again! exclaimed Patri. That's what mom's always telling me. Well she knows what she's talking about, I promise you. How does she know? Inés shrugged her shoulders. They went around the corner and glanced at the building, which didn't look like anything special from the outside.

At that moment, a typical Argentinean beauty walked past: broad weight-lifter's shoulders, pumped-up breasts, narrow hips (viewed from the front, because side-on she was markedly steatopygous), dark skin, almost like an African, indigenous features with certain oriental characteristics, thick protuberant lips, black hair dyed a reddish color, a very short denim skirt showing off her long, strong, lustrous legs, sandals, which she was dragging along languorously, and a key-ring dangling from her hand. Inés and Patri, petite and delicate, slipped past her like two ants beside an elephant. The Argentinean woman didn't even look at them; her big, dark Japanese eyes were half closed, and she wore an expression of disdain. That's what they're like, said Inés Viñas when they were certain distance away. What do they do if they can't get a real man, smack his head off or something? Patri didn't reply, but the image of a real man without a head remained with her for a few steps. Inés added: We don't have that athletic determination . . . and, besides, we can't dress like that, there aren't any clothes that suit us that well. Then Patri said softly: It's because we're different. We're Chilean.

Before going in, Inés pointed out an old red and white van covered with mud, parked on the opposite pavement, a certain distance away. Isn't that Javier's? she asked. Yes, it was. What a wreck! Then both of them thought: They've arrived. A pretty straightforward deduction, really.

Any doubts they might have had disappeared when they went in: an unusual racket of children's voices was echoing down from the top floors. Not that Javier and his wife Carmen had lots of children (they had two and were expecting a third); it was because of the multiplying effect that children produce when they get together. Right now, said Inés, I'd appreciate an elevator. Each of them was carrying a bag of ice. Patri glanced at the electric clock hanging from the beam on the ground floor: it was seven twenty-five. Two ghosts were floating in the air, in line with each of the clock's hands: because of the time, they were both head down, like the branches of a Christmas tree. Come on, or it'll all melt, said Inés. What's the hurry? It's going to melt anyway.

As they climbed the stairs, Patri, who had been thinking about what they had said when the Argentinean woman went past, asked: Don't you think they're more vulgar? Inés Viñas didn't want to be categorical, although it was perfectly obvious what Patri was thinking: Well, my girl, they're different, just like you said. To us they seem primitive, savage, like those tribes ... For example, they have codes of appearance: you can always tell at a glance whether an Argentinean woman is married or single; it's as if they put a bone through their nose when they got married, or shaved their heads, or something like that. But with us ... we all seem married, or all single, if you like. We're always the same. Patri agreed as they climbed the stairs.

The situation on the terrace had changed substantially. The assembly of women had become a general meeting, buzzing with attention, tacit family understandings, news, the roughness of men, and a good quantity of joy. For a start, they had taken some chairs from the dining room to a part of the terrace shaded by the neighboring building. It was even possible to imagine that a cooler breeze was beginning to stir, but that was just the impression naturally created by open air and altitude combined. Here's the ice! cried Raúl Viñas. Javier Viñas stood up to greet the women. He was thinner than his brother, and taller too, although still short, more reserved, more distinguished-looking, but he also smiled more and had a more affectionate manner, although he was not so mysterious; perhaps, all in all, he was more ordinary. He hugged his sister and then addressed an elaborate greeting to Patri, with whom all the family were especially polite. Raúl Viñas had risen to his feet to greet his sister and apologized for having been asleep when she arrived. Carmen Larraín, Javier's wife, also exchanged salutations with her sister-in-law and Patri, while her children, Pablo and Enrique, paragons of politeness, patiently waited their turn. What about Roberto? Carmen asked Inés Viñas.

He'll be right along. They proceeded to talk about him in his absence. Unlike the hosts, Carmen and Javier had met Roberto. They lavished praise upon him, while the interested party expressed prudent reservations. Roberto was a Chilean-Argentinean, a traveling salesman for a small cigarette paper manufacturer. The engagement had been formalized only a few weeks before; they were planning to get married at the end of the coming year, which would begin in a few hours' time. The Viñas brothers (Inés was the youngest child, by a fair margin; Raúl and Javier were twins) were observing the developments with interest. A man's entry into the family was apparently more important than a woman's; they had each brought a woman in already, and in Raúl's case, a prior daughter as well: Patri, that enigmatic supplement. In fact the opposite was true, but the apparent was more important that the real. They considered the prospect at leisure, in a gentle, affectionate, futile way, since it was one of those things that is only a matter of time (which are the things that make time matter). With all the chatting it got quite noisy up there, thirty yards above street level. The presence of the men made a difference: it was more international, not as strictly Chilean as when the women had been talking amongst themselves, less of an artificial enclave, not so much a gathering of exiles, and yet at the same time more Chilean too, in a certain way. Differences like that made the women feel that the men were irreplaceable.

Elisa took the bags into the kitchen, and Carmen Lar-

raín went with her, asking the usual question: Did she
need any help? It was customary to reply in the negative.
Raúl Viñas had suggested that they bring glasses for the
first toast. Your husband's eyes are so red, dear, said Carmen, they're like slices of raw ham. Elisa laughed uproari-
ously. Her sister-in-law was renowned for her witticisms.
In case it wasn't obvious, she explained that he had been
celebrating with his workmates at lunchtime. Ah, well, it's
understandable then. Of course it is! A transition: Tell me,
what are you cooking? Oh, nothing special, chicken, and
the salads there, see what I bought. Perfect, perfect, said
Carmen Larraín without even looking. Who's hungry in
this weather? Hey, what do your kids like? Everything, but
they don't eat much; don't make anything special for them.
You've brought them up so well, your kids, said Elisa Vicuña. Mine just refuse to eat. Wait till they grow a bit, dear.
I guess that's all I can do: wait. They laughed. Patri came in,
like a shadow. Her mother asked her to take out cups for
all the children and put an ice cube in each one. The girl
counted out six orange plastic cups and placed them on a
tray of gold-colored cardboard. The mothers started talking
about Carmen's pregnancy. The experience of pregnancy
was always interesting; though repeated often enough to
be envisaged by all women, it still retained an exceptional
character, which set it apart from, and above, normal repetitions. Outside, the men were talking about oceanography:
the return of the catastrophic El Niño current. The children rushed for the cups, and were disappointed to find that

they contained only little ice cubes, and nothing to drink. Reluctant to waste the opportunity to do something, they started shaking the cups to make a noise, and naturally some ice came out and fell on the floor. Inés Viñas called them to order and took them all to a tap so they could rinse off the cubes, which were covered with dust. Even those who hadn't dropped their ice wanted to rinse it. I'm bringing the Coke, said Patri. Hey, Patricita, bring our glasses, don't forget, will you, said Raúl Viñas. She smiled: Mom brought them already. What a good girl, remarked Javier. The heat seemed to have diminished with the approach of night. Perhaps it hadn't really, but at least the light was not so harsh. Elongated shadows hung in the air above them, and the sun was sinking toward their homeland.

The grown-ups helped themselves to two or three ice cubes each, which they put into the good glasses. They were abundantly served with soft drinks and wine, and began to drink immediately. What about the toast? asked Inés Viñas. The first drink's for thirst, said her brother Raúl. Anyway, remarked Elisa, Roberto still hasn't arrived. Well, said Raúl, accommodatingly, what about we drink an interim toast? Let's just wait for the sweat to break out. His joke was a great success, because they had all noticed that almost as soon as the drink went down their throats, they were wet from head to foot. Apparently it was hotter than they had thought. Or perhaps their bodies had dehydrated without them realizing, and now had to go through a phase of re-adaptation. For a moment all of them, even the children, remained still, dripping with perspiration. The climate of Buenos Aires was different; it still had surprises like this in store, although they had been living in it for years. Elisa went back to the kitchen to start preparing the chicken. The children broke the spell, and began to shout and run around again. A big white piece of paper came floating through the still air from somewhere and fell onto the men. Javier Viñas shook it off, and then examined it. With a few precise movements he folded it into a boat; it was a skill he had perfected. He gave it to the children, who had never played with such a big paper boat and immediately wanted some water to float it in. How could we get enough water? asked Carmen. Put it in the pool, suggested Javier, and when they fill it up, it'll float. So they did, for a bit of fun, and since fun always finds a way to go on, the older cousins climbed down the metal ladder into the pool, although they had been forbidden to do so, on the pretext that the boat had fallen on its side, and they wanted to leave it upright, waiting for the flood. Rock music emerged from a neighboring house.

When Elisa looked out from the kitchen, Raúl Viñas seized the opportunity to propose a first toast. He called his wife, and since there was a general desire to formalize the little ceremony, everyone, including the children, picked up their refilled cups and glasses. All eyes converged on the host, who had lifted his glass and was gazing absently at the wine. We're waiting, said Javier. Raúl Viñas raised his eyebrows, as if he were about to speak, yet a few seconds of silence ensued. Could he have been thinking? Possibly, because when he finally uttered the toast, they were struck by its aptness. He said simply, "To the year." And they all approved. If it had been a year of happiness, it was worth drinking to. And if not, it didn't matter, because the three words had a deeper or higher meaning: the prodigious gift of a year's time, loved and respected by all. But it *had* been a year of happiness, thought Patri, and in that sense the toast concealed a secret, not shared by the others, known only to them, Elisa, Raúl and Patri (the children didn't count, although they were an essential component of the happiness). The others were left out, but they didn't know. It was immediately suggested that the children should also propose toasts, and Patri was invited to open the proceedings, as the oldest member of the next generation, so, without much thought, she said: To my mom and dad. Then, thinking that the last word of the sentence might lead to confusion between her progenitor, "the best man in the world," and Raúl Viñas, she added: "That is, Raúl Viñas." This was considered very fitting; the grown-ups smiled. The children followed her example, each proposing a toast, "To my mom and dad, that is Raúl (or Javier) Viñas," even baby Jacqueline, who babbled it out, parroting the words of her siblings and cousins. The adults listened seriously right to the end, smiling a little as well. Then they knocked back the wine. The conversations began again, with an extra degree of joy and liveliness.

But Patri went on worrying that she had put her foot

in it. She hadn't; on the contrary, if she had been able to read the adults' thoughts, she would have seen that she had their full approval. But it wasn't what she had said that was worrying her so much as a familiar yet troubling anxiety, which had been mounting for a few minutes. It was like approaching the void. She left her glass on the ground and walked over to the edge of the pool, on the bottom of which the giant paper boat was lying, forgotten now, right in the middle, on the dry cement. She walked all the way around the pool until she came to the rear of the building. From there, the sunset was visible, becoming intensely yellow and red. The sun was setting, and the year was setting. The "Year of Happiness," as Raúl Viñas had suggested. They had drunk the sun in one gulp, and the originator of the toast had a special reason for doing so: it wasn't just that he had spent the year drinking, or even that he was going to continue from now until midnight; the reason was that drinking allowed him to stretch time, without in any way altering its punctuality and precision. Also, by virtue of a curious linguistic habit, "New Year" was an instant, twelve midnight, the minute when the sirens went off. And happiness was, precisely, an instant, not a year.

When Patri lowered her eyes, still dazzled from looking directly at the sun, she thought she saw human-shaped shadows flying through the air and into the sixth floor, just below her feet. Who could they be? Her anxiety gave way naturally to a feeling of curiosity, and she could see no reason to suppress it. So she continued her circuit of the pool, walking along the other side now, more quickly, heading for the stairwell. To get there she had to pass in front of the others, who were chatting away noisily, but no one noticed her. She went down the stairs. Although the sixth floor was empty, it seemed different. In the several minutes or half-hour since she had come up with Inés, the configuration of light had changed. The shadows had thickened toward the front, and an intense yellow light was coming in from the back, through the passageways. The perfection of the silence was accentuated by the faint, far-sounding noise of conversation and laughter coming from the terrace above. Paradoxically, a frightening intimation of the unknown was creeping in from the bright side.

Stepping lightly, Patri ventured toward the back. This is not unusual. When a woman, in a film for example, approaches a mysterious room where the bravest spectator wouldn't dare set foot, fear counts for nothing. In this case, it's true, there was no possibility of supernatural danger or any other kind (although the gate in the fence had been left unlocked and unchained). She reached the back landing, onto which the bedroom doors opened; the empty spaces were outlined with strong yellow light. There was not a sound to be heard. She went into the middle room. Somewhat dazzled, she took two steps, and two ghosts passed her saying, "We're in a hurry, a big hurry," then disappeared through the wall. She turned around, went out, and rushed into the adjoining room, so as not to miss them. They were already passing through another wall, and their legs seemed to be sinking into the floor. "Why?" she asked them. She went onto the landing. One of the ghosts had turned toward her. "Why what?" "Why are you in a hurry?" "Because of the party," the ghost replied. They had been tracing a downward curve through space and now they were sinking into the floor and the base of the bathroom wall. "What party?" she asked. Before his head went under, the slower ghost had time to reply: The Big Midnight Feast . . .

Patri rushed to the stairs, realizing there was something entirely new and unprecedented about the ghosts. In her surprise all she could do was hurry, without stopping to think about what they had said. The novelty was precisely that they had spoken to her, and answered her questions.

Although she hated running (and was aware that whatever disappears will reappear), when she got down to the fifth floor, Patri ran to the place where, according to her calculations, the ghosts should have emerged from the ceiling (it still hadn't dawned on her why she was hurrying), but they were already gone. She plotted the curve approximately with her gaze, down to the point where the floor should have swallowed them up. She hesitated for a moment, and then, through a doorframe, saw a group of five or six go by, floating half way between the ceiling and the floor. Although momentary, the vision struck her as even stranger than what she had just seen, almost as if she were in the presence of real men. She took a few steps in the passageway; on this floor there were a number of bedrooms in a row. She could see ghosts in the next bedroom, and in the

third. "Are you going to the party too?" she asked, finally.
One of the ghosts turned his head and said, "Of course,
Patri," but a second later they were disappearing through
the wall. These ghosts were moving along a curve as well,
but it would only have been visible from above, since they
were maintaining a constant altitude. They passed briefly
through the corner of the third bedroom, and came out
into the big living room at the back, which was flooded
with light. There the velocity of their movement increased.
Patri got her first good look at them, as they traced an
increasingly rapid arc in front of her. "Why did you say
'of course'?" she asked, continuing the conversation. A different ghost, not the one who had spoken before, asked
in turn, "Who'd miss the Big Midnight Feast?" but didn't
look at her (indeed he seemed to be facing the opening at
the back, the source of light). And when they were already
disappearing through the wall on the left, she heard one of
their characteristic peals of laughter, which, for some reason, sounded incongruous now. She wanted to ask who was
throwing the party, but was too shy. Instead she followed
their circular path all the way to the big living room at the
front (corresponding to the one at the back) where they
scattered like a squadron of fighter planes.

Since she had ended up near the stairs, and various
ghosts had been following downward paths, she decided
to go down to the next floor. From one floor to the next,
the light diminished. Since fewer partition walls had gone
up on the fifth floor, she could see through to the back,

where some of the ghosts were floating in empty space,
beyond the edge. It wasn't really accurate to say that they
were floating. It looked to her more like they were standing, on something that could not be seen. She went toward
them, with a sleepwalker's clear innocence. And they were
watching her.

There was something architectural about the dusk as
well. It was a construction, not governed by chance, as one
might have supposed in the case of a meteorological phenomenon, but well thought out; or rather, it was itself a
kind of thought. The largest conceivable spaces were transformed into instants, and under covering layers like roofs
or paving stones, grids of shadows, light and color formed.
But it couldn't be called a real construction, not in the usual
sense of the word, not as the building was real, for example.
The dusk was provisional, indifferent, subtle; its compart-
ments of light were home to no one, for the moment, but
anyone could see their image cut out of a photograph and
stuck to the beautiful heavenly roof. Within the imaginary
Great Construction, minor, real constructions reared, glori-
ously useless and incomplete, provisional too, but in their
own way, hinting at permanence. And the strangest thing
about it was that all this was a time of day, or night, but
really more a time of day, and nothing else.

Absorbed by the sight of the ghosts, Patri had come almost too close to the edge. When she realized this, she took
a step back. She observed them in the half-light, although
they were a little too high, relative to her line of sight, for

her to study them in detail. She could tell that they were the same as ever; what had changed was the light. She had never seen them so late in the day, not in summer. The unreal look they had in the saturated light of siesta-time, at once so shocking and so reassuring, like idiotic bobbing toys, had evaporated in the dramatic half-light of evening. They rose up in front of her quite slowly; but, given her previous experiences, Patri had reason to believe that their slowness was swarming with a variety of otherworldly speeds. Seen from the right distance, what seemed almost as slow as the movement of a clock's hand could turn out to be something more than mere high velocity; it could be the very flow of light or vision.

In this new, late apparition, their bodies had become three-dimensional, tangible; and what bodies they were, such depth and strength! The dust that covered them had become a splendid decoration; now that it didn't have to absorb tremendous quantities of sunlight, it allowed the dark golden color of their skin to show through, and accentuated their musculature, the perfection of their surfaces. Here were the bulging pectorals she thought she had seen in normal, living men, the well-proportioned arms, the symmetrically sculpted abdomens, the long smooth legs. And their genital equipment, somewhat curved, but also slightly raised by the sheer force of its own bulk (it's true she was looking from below), was different from anything she had seen, as if more real, more authentic.

They watched her as they rose, since they were rising

and moving forward, toward the fifth floor, at the rear of the building. They looked down at her and smiled an inde-cipherable smile.

Who's throwing the party?

We are.

They were no longer laughing as if possessed. They were speaking, with warm voices and words she could un-derstand, in a Spanish without accent, neither Chilean nor Argentinean, like on television. They were speaking to her, and it was like being addressed by television characters. She was even more surprised by the way they seemed to be rational. Her surprise crystallized the feeling that had made her come downstairs; that vague, indefinite worry and alarm were becoming a specific torment, a pain, which was inde-finable too, but for different reasons, as if it were impossible for her to touch the most genuine reality, the reality of a promise that eluded her grasp. Not that the ghosts had aroused her desires; that was, of course, impossible; and yet, in another sense, they had. Some desires, while less exact and practical, are no less urgent, or even less sexual. She told herself she shouldn't have heeded her curiosity, she should have resisted. But it was useless. She would do it again, a thousand times, as long as she lived.

They had disappeared over her head. The last she saw of them were their heels. She had tipped her head so far back that when she reassumed her normal posture she felt dizzy and teetered perilously on the brink, which she had approached again unawares. She turned around and headed for the stairs, intending to go up. In the darkest part of the apartment, at the front, a ghost appeared before her, moving diagonally (which seemed to be the fashion) and upward. It reached the roof before she came near and began to pass through it head first, slowly. So slowly that it seemed to stop halfway through the process (mutations within the movement transferred the velocities to other dimensions). When Patri got there, the bottom half of the ghost's body was hanging from the concrete ceiling, like some dark, nondescript object. She climbed the stairs and went to the rear of the building again, where she had a feeling they would be gathering in greater numbers. And as it turned out, a large group was waiting for her, or seemed to be, by the edge, but outside, in empty space, bathed in the last light, against a background of intense, end-of-evening air. Within the dark visibility of that air they were waiting for her, specifically for her, because one of them called her by name. What? asked Patri, stopping three yards away.

Don't you want to come to our party tonight?

If you invite me . . .

That's what we're doing

A silence. Patri was trying to understand what they had said. Finally she asked:

Why me?

She was bound to ask that. They didn't answer. All things considered, they couldn't. They left her to work it out for herself. There followed a somewhat longer silence.

So?

I'm thinking it over.

Ah.

There seemed to be something ironic in their attitude. They began to withdraw, without making the slightest movement, like visions affected by a shift in perspective. Nevertheless they withdrew, treating the innocent explorer to a sight that could not have been more extraordinary. As if inadvertently, they were entwined by a kind of luminous helix, enveloping them in invisible yellow. The dust on their skin was barely a hint now, a down. At the sight of those men, Patri could feel her heart contracting . . . as if she were truly seeing men for the first time. Stop! cried her soul. Don't go, ever! She wanted to see them like that for all eternity, even if eternity lasted an instant, especially if it lasted an instant. That was the only eternity she could imagine. Come, eternity, come and be the instant of my life! she exclaimed to herself.

Of course you'll have to be dead, said one of them.

That doesn't matter at all, she replied straight away, passionately. Her passion meant something apart from her words, something else, of which she was unaware. But it also meant exactly what she had said.

They seemed to be very still as they watched her. But were they? Perhaps they were traveling at an incredible speed, traversing worlds, and she was in a position from which that movement could not be perceived. That didn't matter either, she thought. In any case, they slid fluidly down to the next floor, leaving her there looking out into the emptiness, where the big city was, and the streets with their lights coming on.

Since she found that spectacle uninteresting, she turned around and went back to the stairs. But when she reached the landing, she realized that she didn't know whether to go up or down to find them again. It was as if, having accomplished their mission, they had disappeared. Anyway, there was no point chasing them up and down the stairs. It would just tire her our and make her legs hurt. You had to really watch your step on those bare cement stairs without banisters. She'd already had plenty of exercise for one day. And, with every passing minute, the exercise of going up and down was becoming more dangerous. The first dense shadows, still shot with glimmers of transparency, were occupying the building.

A shudder ran through Patri's body. Her legs were shaking, but not because of the stairs, or even because of the thickening darkness. She felt dazed. She went down two steps, then sat. There was something she'd been meaning to reflect on, and after sitting for a moment, she was able to give it some serious thought. Except that since she was, as her mother said, "frivolous," she never thought seriously about anything. And in this case her frivolity was exacerbated by the subject of her would-be serious reflections, which was something quintessentially frivolous: a party.

But in a way parties were serious and important too, she thought. They were a way of suspending life, all the serious business of life, in order to do something unimportant:

and wasn't that an important thing to do? We tend to think of time as taking place within time itself, but what about when it's outside? It's the same with life: normal, daily life, which can seem to be the only admissible kind, conceived within the general framework of life itself. And yet there were other possibilities, and one of them was the party: life outside life.

Was it possible to decline an invitation to a party? Patri wondered. Leaving aside the specious argument according to which, if an invitation, like the one she had just received, came from outside life, simply to hear it was to accept, it clearly *was* possible to decline. People did it every day. But how many such invitations could you expect to receive in a lifetime? As well as the vertical stratification of life into layers or doors through which one could "enter" or "exit," there was a "horizontal" or temporal axis, which measured the duration of a life. Invitations to a magic party with ghosts were obviously going to be very rare. There might be another chance, but for Patri that was beside the point. She was wondering how many such invitations there could be in eternity. That was a different question. Repetition in eternity was not a matter of probabilities, no matter how large the numbers. In eternity, as distinct from "in life" or "outside life," this party was an absolutely unique occasion.

All these questions came to her wrapped in another: Why not simply accept? And that was where life came back into the picture, denser than ever. Life had an annoying way of setting dates for everything, using time to hollow things out, until what had been compact became as diffuse as a cloud. For a frivolous girl like her, life should have been a solid block, a chunk of marble. Even thought could take on that quality, if the gaps between the elements of the proposition were eliminated. Frivolity is saying four is four. Seriousness is gradually deduced, fraction by tiny fraction, from such moderately useful statements as "two plus two is four," until one arrives at "Columbus discovered America." Frivolity is the tautological effect, produced by *everything* (because you can't be selectively frivolous: it's an all-or-nothing affair). It's the condition of knowing it all in advance, because everything is repetition of itself, tautology, reflection. To be frivolous, then, is to go sliding over those repetitions, supported by nothing else. What else was there? For Patri, nothing.

And yet she hadn't lied when she had said that she was "thinking it over." Thinking is also opening a gap, but, in her case, it was inevitable; she considered herself almost as an object of thought, someone else's thought, of course, and someone remote at that. The ghosts put her in a position where she had to think, had to attend to thinking.

But not because there was something to think over: as always, the decision had already been taken, automatically. Of course she would go. And they must have known she would, which is why they stuck to the essentials and dispensed with the customary practice of praising the party in advance. She would go. She didn't even feel the need to make a list of all her reasons for going.

The sound of footsteps interrupted her reasoning; she couldn't tell if they were coming from above or below. She lifted her head, but couldn't see much; night had fallen. The voices of her family up on the terrace carried clearly, as if they were within arm's reach. The steps sounded almost like whispers. Finally she realized that someone or something was coming up the flight of stairs immediately below the one on which she was sitting. She got to her feet, but didn't have time to turn around and go up, as she had intended, because a shadow appeared on the landing and began to climb, apparently still unaware of her presence. It was only when that shadow reached the midpoint of the flight of stairs that the light coming in through the hazardous gaps in the flooring around the staircase allowed her to see more clearly. It was a man about thirty years old, and the best-looking man she had ever seen in her life: white T-shirt, white moccasins, cream-colored trousers with well-ironed creases, gold watch and necklace, a ring with a red stone, bulging biceps emerging from his short sleeves, a pony-tail but the rest of his hair trimmed fashionably short, in a South American "pudding bowl" cut, with no sideburns, aerodynamic wrap-around sunglasses, and a cigarette in the corner of his mouth. He smiled at her languidly:

You must be Patri.

She couldn't even open her mouth. She had no idea who this gentleman could be, or how he knew who she was.

I'm Roberto.

Roberto? she asked, as she would squirm to remember later on: it was such an impolite question, almost as bad as saying: What Roberto?

But he wasn't offended. He chuckled, stepped forward, took her by the arm, and up they went. Inés Viñas's boyfriend, he said. Ah, Roberto, cried Patri, blushing so deeply that, if not for the darkness, she would have looked like a tomato—but this individual, with his sunglasses, could probably see in the dark. Am I late? No sir, I don't think dinner has been served yet. He laughed again, and asked her please not to be so formal. Call me Roberto, he said.

It was nine. There were various signs that dinner was imminent, including the smell of roast chicken and its effect on the guests. In the absence of a miracle, it had, predictably, turned out to be one of those oppressively hot Buenos Aires nights, exactly like the day, but without light. The children had restricted the ambit of their games and cries to the lighted area, with occasional escapes and chases into the darkness, from which they soon returned to the center of their fun. This made them more annoying than before, but also gave the whole gathering a more joyful and intimate feel, as if they were all enclosed in a room without walls. In the darkness, the red and blue toy cars looked the same. A bare light globe over the dining-room door was all the lighting they had, and all they needed. A few mosquitoes and moths traced their paths through the zones of light. Raúl Viñas remarked that one advantage of living so high up was that not many flying critters came to visit. There were none of the insects that precede a storm. The conversation continued, fluidly, in grand style. Conversation was paramount. The presence of men changed its nature, not so much because they focused on particular themes; it was more that they altered the form of the exchange, with their emphatic affirmations and deeply misguided ideas about everyday matters. Generally, the women acknowledged this difference, and appreciated it, especially since they had so few opportunities to talk all together: only at family gatherings like this one, or meetings called to resolve a particular issue, but in that case they weren't as free to change the subject. Still, the women went on speaking amongst themselves, under cover of the general conversation, even sending each other subtle signals, which were received with little smiles here and there.

The appearance of Roberto caused a sensation. They all agreed that he wasn't like they had imagined him. Not that he was better or worse: different. But that was just because he had really appeared. Even Carmen and Javier, who already knew him, had imagined him differently. He seemed Argentinean, which could be explained by the fact that he was, partly; although, of course, he was far more Chilean than Argentinean. Inés looked at him with surprise when he arrived: Hadn't he brought anything? The bottles of wine? The ice cream? But weren't you going to bring them? he asked, looking even more surprised. There had been a misunderstanding. After all that discussion about what they should bring to the party! They had made careful, considered decisions, but then they got mixed up about who was to bring it all. Soon everyone was laughing about it. Especially Elisa Vicuña. Roberto was nice and very polite. Raúl Viñas invited him to sit down with them—him and Javier—and they started talking. He took off his dark glasses, revealing small green eyes, the eyes of a good boy. You don't look Chilean! exclaimed Carmen, while her husband expressed the opposite opinion. There are so many kinds of Chileans! said Elisa. That's what I always say, added Roberto.

His arrival allowed Patri's absence to go unnoticed. But not entirely, because when she came into the kitchen, once all the fuss of greeting the boyfriend was over, Inés, who was apologizing again to her sister-in-law for the mix-up, asked: Where have you been, kid? Just around, she replied, without going into details. Her mother glanced across at her. Who knows where she got to, off in some mysterious dream-world of her own, probably. Your boyfriend is so good-looking, Elisa said to Inés Viñas. Do you think? Oh yes!

The table had to be taken out, so the men went to do it, or rather the brothers, since they wouldn't let Roberto help. But the table, as it turned out, didn't want to go through the kitchen door. They couldn't tell if it was because alcohol and nightfall combined had befuddled them, or if there was a geometrical difficulty; in any case it proved to be difficult, indeed apparently impossible. If it went in, said Javier Viñas, it must be possible to get it out. But *did* it go in? asked

Raúl Viñas, joking at first, but then, almost straight away, his mind was thrown into confusion by a panicky doubt, as he wondered whether the table hadn't been put in the dining room before the walls went up. He remembered putting up those walls, but at the time, he could have sworn, they were living on the ground floor. Just then, while he was still in a daze, having got two of the legs out, he tilted the table top slightly, and it came through, to unanimous applause. They put it in what seemed like the best place, neither too far from the door (that is, the light) nor too close. Half-light is always pleasant for dining, but the heat made it even more intimate and mystical. The adults, seven if Patri was included in the count, fitted around it perfectly. They set up a low table for the children, with planks and trestles, as they generally did for more formal meals: a kind of long coffee table, like the one the builders threw together for their lunchtime barbecues downstairs. Seating was the problem. The family's four chairs and four benches were sufficient only for the adults. The solution was to take another leaf from the builders' book: they could go down and fetch the boxes they sat on every day at lunchtime. All three of the men went, none of them wanting to seem less polite, but also because several arms would be required. They set off joyfully, following Raúl Viñas's torch.

Meanwhile, Patri was busy setting the table. First she spread a pretty white table cloth, and the rest happened almost automatically: plates, forks, knives. As for the glasses, which the men had left on the floor, she had a supernatural knack for guessing who they belonged to, and she never made a mistake. In the kitchen, Iñes Viñas and her two sisters-in-law were preparing the salads, and of course chatting. The main topic was Roberto, considered from various points of view, but one in particular. The unspoken question behind all the remarks, which were magically transformed into preemptive replies, was: How did Inés Viñas avoid getting pregnant? She seemed to be wondering too, as if she didn't trust her own thoughts or her life.

Elisa had put a melon into a tureen full of ice cubes, to cool it down. Inés had made an innovative suggestion: wrap it in wet newspaper first, then cover it with ice, so it would cool more quickly. The result was sensational. The green and white rind was frosted. Elisa worked out when the chickens would be done. When it came to timing, she was an expert and she liked the courses to follow one another fairly rapidly; the children were happier that way, and it meant her husband had less idle time for drinking.

Well, now they could begin. Carmen Larraín went out to ask the men if they were ready. Of course they were, ready and waiting! Just one thing: there were no napkins. She came back to the kitchen with the message, and Patri raised a hand to her forehead: how could she have forgotten? She always did. Her mother told her to check on the children once she had put the napkins out. Meanwhile Elisa was serving the melon, with the help of Inés Viñas, placing the slices on a long platter, and covering each one with a sliver of ham. Carmen and Patri went to quiet the children down. Juan

Sebastián, who had been appointed head of the table, was barking despotic orders, mainly at his siblings (he was slightly afraid of his cousins, with their disciplined air).

The melon arrived, and the cook sat down: the meal was beginning. There were two slices each for the grown-ups, and one (cut in two) for the children. It wasn't real sustenance yet, just a treat to whet the appetite. It's important to remember that, for this family, food was not a major concern. They gave it almost no consideration. The melon was perfectly ripe; had they eaten it a day later (or a day earlier), it wouldn't have been the same. The sweetness, with all its exquisite intensity, did not detract from the particular flavor of melon, which was not, in itself, sweet at all. And the ham was perfect too; it had a kind of salty warmth that contrasted aptly with the icy sweetness of the fruit. After the melon came the salads, and then, almost immediately, the chickens: perfectly golden, crisp, and moderately seasoned. To accompany the poultry, Raúl Viñas had put aside some bottles of aged Santa Carolina, which he bought at a good price from his favorite wine store. Chilean wines are so dry! they all said, sipping it, with a touch of nostalgia, which they reined in so as not to spoil the evening. They're so dry, so dry! Paradoxically, that dryness filled their eyes with tears. But overall, the meal was a thoroughly joyful occasion; sometimes, in order for joy to be complete, a discreet trace of sadness is required. In any case, the children were well behaved.

The only one who had a secret thought was Patri. Less

an idea than a feeling: she felt that she still had to do something; that there was some unfinished business. What she
really wanted was to stop thinking. She didn't like feeling
that she was a mechanism performing a function, but since
she had told the ghosts that she "had to think about it," she
felt obliged to do so. By nature she was particularly taci-
turn, but this predicament helped her to see the usefulness
of speaking. When you speak, you automatically stop thinking; it's like being released from a contract. Or rather, as she
said to herself, it's like those stories in which an especially
handsome man appears, to whom the virile protagonist
feels inexplicably attracted, which he finds disturbing, understandably, until it is finally revealed that the handsome
man is in fact a woman in disguise. Such is the dialectic
of thinking and speaking. But having reached this point in
her reflections, Patri wondered if she wasn't herself (and this
was the secret of all her thought) a woman in disguise, bril-
liantly disguised . . . as a woman. But she didn't go down
those mysterious passageways, preferring to remain on the
surface of her frivolity, because there was also a dialectical
relation between thought and secrecy. Or, more pertinently
in this case, between thought and time. It simply wasn't possible to go on thinking all the time. It would be like a painter
who has to delay the completion of a picture for technical
reasons, say to allow certain thick layers of color to dry, and
meanwhile is assailed by new ideas—a figure, a mountain, an
animal, and so on—which go on filling up the painting until
the pressure of multiplicity makes it explode.

The children kept escaping from their little table. Stunned by the bliss of the meal, their parents let them be, except when they strayed out of the circle of variably feeble light shed by the globe, because the darkness beyond hid the irrevocable edges of the void, and those of the deep swimming pool, which were dangerous if not so terrible. When they did stray, one of the women would volunteer to go and bring them back, or frighten them into submission with a scolding if that was sufficient. Patri, lost in thought while all the others had gone rounding up the children, was the last to take her turn. There had been a veritable exodus, and some stern words from Elisa had failed to bring them all back to their places, so Patri pushed her chair back and went into the darkness to see what she could see. She walked toward the back of the terrace, to the left of the pool, until she heard the older children running around the right side to get away. But she went all the way to the back anyway, to make sure there were none left. There were no children, and once she was close to the edge, she could see more clearly, because of the light coming up from the houses and the streets. She stopped on the brink, but was not in any danger, because of her pensive mood: she was continually stopping to think, and that moment was no exception. Some ghosts appeared, floating in the air two or three yards away. Night had made them majestic, monumental, perhaps because they were illuminated from below by the glow coming from the Avenida Alberdi on the other side of the block, and they looked like foreshort-

ened figures, barely a few golden lines in the darkness. They
seemed more serious too, but there was no way to be sure.
In Patri's eyes, at any rate, they had entered a spacious do-
main of seriousness. For her, those volumes swimming in
shadow, those volumes reduced to lines, as if to suggest that
they existed in a dimension of aggravated unreality, seemed
strangely, almost incredibly, solemn. The shadows served a
different function for the ghosts, since they had "nothing
to hide" (because they weren't alive). I accept the invitation, said Patri. A minute before midnight I'll jump off here.
Here? asked one of the ghosts, as if he had not heard. Yes,
here. Ah. It's more practical, said Patri, feeling obliged to
explain. Then they nodded; and that simple movement, in-
dicating that they had heard, made them seem less serious.
One of them said: Thank you for the confirmation, young
lady. Everything is ready for the feast.

When she came back to the table, she noticed that her
mother was looking at her strangely, and wondering briefly
what she was thinking. Over the chicken bones and empty
salad bowls, the diners were speaking of this and that. By
a curious coincidence, all of them, without exception, had
been born in the city of Santiago, the most beautiful city in
the world, as they readily agreed, having already made up
their minds. The way they praised Santiago, they could have
been employed by a travel agency.

It's a pity you can't see the stars in Santiago, because of
the smog, said Roberto. I've seen them, said Raúl Viñas,
leaning forward. Under close observation, some of Raúl

Viñas' mannerisms, such as a certain way of swaying his head, could seem to be typical of a drunkard. But it happened that his brother, who didn't drink, or never to excess, had the same mannerisms. So the observer's judgment had to be revised: they were family traits. Roberto was constantly making this readjustment when he spoke with his future brothers-in-law. I've *seen* them, said Raúl Viñas, leaning forward and exaggerating the swaying movement of his head. Yeah, all right, very clever, replied his sister's boyfriend, I've seen them too, otherwise how would I know they exist? I didn't discover them in Argentina. But I saw them in the old days, when I was a kid. I've seen them just recently, said Raúl Viñas. And his brother Javier repeated his words. Listen Roberto, they said, Listen . . . (Right from the start they had decided to dispense with formalities, since they were going to be brothers-in-law; and the women had done the same. Otherwise Roberto would have felt uncomfortable.) Since they weren't agreeing about what they had seen in Santiago, they moved on to not agreeing about something closer to hand. The same thing happens here, said Inés Viñas, although there's no smog. It's because there's too much street lighting. Some people think you can't have enough, Carmen pointed out. But you can see them here too! said Javier Viñas. Don't you believe it, Roberto replied. Hey kids, let's do a test, cried Elisa, then she asked the children to behave, because it was going to be dark for a while. She went to the kitchen, and switched off the light. They all threw their heads back and looked up. When their pupils dilated, an immense starry sky, the whole Milky Way in its rare magnificence, appeared before them. You can hardly see it, said Raúl Viñas. I can see it clear as anything, said Javier. Yes, it's true. Yes, yes. They all looked up and abandoned the conversation. There are the galaxies! said Javier's children. If only we had a telescope!

While the others were going into raptures about the stars, Patri felt that she could see her family in the sky, her beloved family, and realized that she was bidding them farewell. It wasn't true what they said about the dead being turned into stars for the living to see: it was the other way around. She couldn't say that she was sad to be leaving them for ever, but she saw them scattered over the black sky, each a beautiful, everlasting point of light, and felt a kind of nostalgia, not in anticipation but almost as if she were looking back already. She was telling herself that as long as a sacrifice is worthwhile, it is possible. The thing is, the stars were so far away . . . The kids were right: they needed a telescope; but that would have made them look even more distant. She moved her head slightly, and felt that the stars, remote as they were, had entered her. The "state of farewell" implied a certain detachment. That detachment or doubling affected thought as well, and under its influence Patri conceived the following analogy. In the course of his everyday activities, it occurs to a man that in an ideal state of perfect happiness, satisfying all the requirements set out by the philosophers (and some have been extremely particular in these matters, not so much because they were naturally fussy, although they were, because most of them were bachelors, but mainly because they got carried away by their ontological deductions), he would be doing exactly what he is doing now, not something equivalent, but the very same thing, as if in a parallel world. Of course not if his work was really terrible, as so much work is, but these days, thought Patri, quite a few people live without working, so the objects of this man's hypothetical comparisons would be a walk, a session at the gym, a train trip to the suburbs, that sort of thing, and it wouldn't require a great imaginative effort to arrive at the conclusion that there could indeed be a perfect identity between what he is doing in reality, and what he would be doing at the same time, on the same day, in a state of perfect happiness (individual, social and even cosmic happiness, if you like, the end of alienation, etc. etc.). In fact it wouldn't require any imaginative effort at all, because there would be no need to call on the imagination; all he'd have to do would be to modify his gestures, or their form: slightly slower movements, a conceited little smile, the head held slightly higher . . . It's always the way, she thought: you look up at the starry sky, and before you know it you're thinking about other worlds. How idiotic!

Of course, the stars over Santiago, said Javier, are completely different. What do you mean different? he was asked in surprise and bewilderment. They're not the same, he replied. Appalled, Raúl Viñas put his head in his hands. What a dumb thing to say! We're in the same hemisphere! What's that got to do with it? Neither brother knew whether to credit the other's implausible ignorance or assume it was an exercise in mutual leg-pulling. The women laughed. Elisa Vicuña, who was justly reputed for her intelligence, backed up her brother-in-law: But they *are* different. It's true, said Roberto, supporting her. Raúl Viñas had no choice but to yield, mainly because, on that point, he actually was in agreement. Of course they're different, he said, but that doesn't mean they're not the same constellations, the same arrangements, the same stars, if you like. They all looked very carefully at the stars. Was there anything familiar about them? They couldn't say there was, but they couldn't say there wasn't either. What I think, said Patri, is that they're the same but back to front. *Exactly*, said Raúl, Patricita is right. Point of view is everything, said Carmen. And to think we've seen those stars from the other side, said Inés Viñas, poised between melancholy and delight. But their necks had begun to hurt, and since the children had taken advantage of the darkness to escape and tear around like little devils, they switched on the light again. They emerged from that plunge into the starry darkness smiling more broadly, and saw each other with different eyes, which were, of course, logically, the same. They drank a toast: To the stars of Chile. There's a current that carries the stars away! said Raúl Viñas, between mouthfuls.

Soon the fruit was served and they were tasting it. All the family preferred fruit to desserts, which was lucky for the mistress of the household, because it meant less work, although she still had to peel, pit, and remove seeds, especially for the children. When they told Roberto, he couldn't believe it. It turned out that he was exactly the same. His devotion to fruit was matched only by his aversion to desserts; serving them after the finest meal was enough to spoil all the pleasure retrospectively. He was sure that Inés must have mentioned it, that quirk of his, but no, on the contrary, Elisa Vicuña had been worried that he wouldn't be satisfied with plain fruit, served in the primitive style. Even so she hadn't wanted to spoil the rest of the family's pleasure. It was almost telepathic, a coincidence that proved he was meant to be part of the family. And what fruit! Glorious nectarines, so ripe they were violet, mosque-shaped apricots, bunches of green and black grapes, each one sublime, bleeding strawberries, Anjou pears with snow-white flesh, purple cherries, big black plums, all the abundance of nature, civilized to a supreme degree of refinement by grafting and husbandry, to the point where any improvement in flavor would almost have been imperceptible. Nothing less could satisfy this family of insatiable fruit-eaters; luckily fruit was cheap in summer.

Did you know, said Elisa, that we have ghosts on this site? Real ghosts? they asked. Well, they're never real, are they? But you can see them, every day, at siesta time. And other times, added Patri. Yes, other times too. The conversation moved on to ghosts. Everyone could contribute an experience, a memory, or at least something they had heard. It was the ideal subject for storytelling.

Raúl Viñas told the story of the ghost who was walking

along and, distracted by the sight of a plane flying over, fell into a well. In the well there was a hare, and they struck up a conversation. The hare (a male hare, while the ghost, as it happened, was the ghost of a woman) had also fallen in by accident, and had stayed there, not because he couldn't get out (it wasn't a very deep well) but to rest. Were you watching the plane flying over too? asked the ghost. No, said the hare, I was running away. Uh huh? said the ghost, her curiosity piqued. What from? The hare shrugged his shoulders, difficult as that may be to imagine. He went on to explain that in fact he was always running away, from everything, so in the end he didn't really distinguish between reasons for flight. But you should, advised the ghost. Why? said the hare. Why run away more quickly from what seems to be more dangerous, and more slowly from what seems a lesser threat? That would be a grave mistake, because you can always judge wrongly, and even if you don't, the lesser threat could turn out to be fatal. The ghost concurred, and said reflectively that it had been rash of her to offer advice on a subject she knew nothing about. Understandably enough, since her specialty—appearing—was the opposite of flight. The hare sighed, envying his chance companion's lot: how wonderful not to have to worry about preserving your life! Except that you have to start by losing it, the ghost remarked wisely. Ah, but then . . . You see . . . No, sorry, but you're mistaken . . . Allow me to . . . They were so absorbed in their philosophizing that they didn't notice the arrival of a hunter, a bad sport as we shall see, and inept too, who looked over the edge of the well, and seeing a defenseless hare at his feet, cocked his shotgun (that sinister "click" finally brought the hare and the ghost back down to earth, but all they had time to do was freeze), and fired: bang. Since he was a poor shot, he hit the ghost, who of course he hadn't seen. Transparent as air, blood spurted from a wound on the left side of her chest. The hare had no time to pity her, since, like the classic moral at the end of a fable, he had leapt out of the well with a single bound, and was already far away, fleeing as fast as he could.

Javier Viñas told the story of the old watchmaker who could tell what time it was by observing the positions of ghosts, which led him, by association, to depressing reflections on the decline of his trade. All things analog were losing ground, and the tendency seemed to be irreversible. It saddened him to hear people say "Eleven fifty-six, seven thirty-nine, two-o-one" as they walked past his poky little shop. Nobody said "it's just gone twenty to two" because even a child would have replied, "You mean one forty-one? Or one forty-two?" Now his only clients were little old men like himself with some broken-down antique, an Omega, a Vacheron Constantin, or a Girard Perregaux, and he was no longer surprised when one of them decided that it wasn't worth repairing, and walked past the next day with a Japanese watch on his wrist. Soon no one would know that the hour is made up of two halves. Already the ticking of a watch was a thing of the past: the heart was an outmoded organ. Because the ticking of a watch was "like" that of the heart; in other words, they were analogs. And analog watches were the old ones, the ones with hands. It was true that there were also imitation analog watches, with hands, which operated digitally, but that was ostentatious or condescending, and gave the old watchmaker little hope. He spent the day sitting still, feeling depressed, stiller and more depressed each day, staring at the back wall of the shop, where two ghosts showed the time, all day long. They were two child-sized ghosts, so punctual and patient that the watchmaker found it natural for them to be there, showing the time. And the stiller he became, the more natural the slow, sure movement of the ghost-hands seemed. But he shouldn't have been so complacent. Because one afternoon, the ghosts came down from their places and said to him with a mischievous smile: Time passes, you stupid old miser, technology changes, but not human greed, and "backwards" people like you just spread gloom, which has spoilt life for ghosts. Aren't you ashamed? The old watchmaker was so astonished, he couldn't even open his mouth. He felt himself being swept up by an impalpable force, into the air, and carried to that place by the back wall where the ghosts had shown the time. Now he was showing it, his body marking the hour, as on the first clock faces, before the invention of the minute hand. Meanwhile the real ghosts had vanished.

Not to be outdone, the women told ghost stories too. Inés Viñas told the story of a portraitist who abandoned his art as a result of specializing in ghost portraits. The ghosts materialized only to pose and then disappeared again. It was frustrating for the artist not to have any enduring reality with which to compare his work. But that was not the worst thing. The worst thing was that the ghosts rationed their visibility in a rather drastic manner, and didn't even materialize in their entirety; only the feature that the artist was copying at a particular moment appeared, and not even that: just the line, the mere brush-stroke . . . They duplicated his work so perfectly that the exasperated painter broke his brushes, stamped on his palette, kicked the easel over, and bought himself a Leica. Which only made things worse, much worse.

As for Carmen Larraín, she told them about Japanese ghosts. In the Celestial Empire, when an elder died, there was a general reckoning of where he had left the bones on the plate every time he ate fish. If the positions formed a satisfactory circle, he went to Paradise. If not, he became a ghost whose task was to teach the children good table manners. And those who did not succeed in that mission, she concluded, became ikebana instructors.

Finally, instead of telling a story, Roberto made an observation: ghosts, he said, are like dwarves. Thinking about them in abstract terms, you could come to the conclusion that they don't exist, and depending on the kind of life you lead, you can go for months or years without seeing one, but sooner or later, when you least expect it, there they are. That's just a result of life's general conditions, the chances and coincidences that make up existence; for example, it can happen that in a single day, you see two dwarves, or two dozen, and then you don't see any more for the rest of the year. Now looking at it from the other side, from the dwarf's point of view, the situation's very different, because the dwarf is always present to himself, as he is: 44 inches tall, with his big head, and his short, bandy legs. He is the occasion that prompts casual passersby to say, that night: "Today I saw a dwarf." But for him, dwarfhood is constant, continual, and merits no special remark. It's perpetual appearing, occasion transformed into life and destiny.

Isn't Patricita going to tell us a story? they asked, looking at her; it was true that she hadn't said a word. The children had approached the table and were listening to the stories with gaping mouths. Patri thought for a moment before speaking: I remember a story by Oscar Wilde, about a princess who was bored in her palace, bored with her parents, the king and queen, bored with the ministers, the generals, the chamberlains, and the jesters, whose jokes she knew by heart. One day a delegation of ghosts appeared to invite her to a party they were giving on New Year's Eve, and their descriptions of this party, which included the disguises they would wear and the music to be played by the ghost orchestra, were so seductive, and she was so bored, that without a second thought that night she threw herself from the castle's highest tower, so that she could die and go to the party. The others pondered the moral. So the story doesn't say what happened at the party? asked Carmen Larraín. No. That's where it stops. Must have been a bit of a surprise for the girl! said Elisa, giggling. Why? Because ghosts are gay, of course! Raucous guffaws. That Oscar Wilde, he's priceless! said Roberto, choking with laughter. They all thought Elisa Vicuña's reply was a great joke, in the surrealist mode. An inspired one-liner. Patri, however, only laughed so that they wouldn't think she was upset; the idea had shocked and distressed her. At that moment, the children were pointing at the moon, which had been rising in the sky, partly hidden by the neighboring buildings, partly eclipsed by the absorbing conversation. They all looked up. It reminded them that they were dining outdoors. It was a very white full moon, without haloes, the kind of moon you could spend your life watching, except that in life the moon is always changing.

When Elisa got up to prepare the coffee, Patri was quick to follow her into the kitchen, saying "I'll give you a hand." The rest of them went on talking and drinking wine. Raúl Viñas drank four glasses in the time it took the others to finish one. The result was an exquisite inebriation that went unnoticed in social situations, but sent his whole body into orbit, endowing it with a peculiar movement, shifting it to places where no one thought it was. Once they were alone, Patri asked what Elisa had meant by the quip that had gone down so well. But, my girl . . . her mother began, and here the expression "my girl," so common in the familiar speech of Chileans, so normal that even daughters sometimes use it without thinking when addressing their mothers, also took on a broader sense, which neutralized the typically Chilean connotations. The language shifted to its most abstract level, almost as if Elisa were speaking on television: But my girl, we never know what we mean, and even if we did, it wouldn't matter. You're always saying things don't matter, said Patri, in a slightly reproachful tone, which, as always in their conversations, was tempered with affection. But as Elisa put the water on to boil, spooned the coffee into the pot, passed the cups to her daughter so that she could check they were clean and put them on the tray with the saucers and the little spoons, she became very serious. There were things she needed to say to her daughter, things that really did matter. They had spoken so much, half-jokingly, about the "real men" who were destined to make them happy, and they had made light of them so often, that in their respective imaginations, the subject had lost its gravity. She had to restore it, by reasoning if need be, and there was no time like the present, now, before the end of the year. How can I tell you, she said to her daughter, then stopped and thought. Patricita, I'm afraid you're not the most observant member of the family. Come on, tell me, tell me, said her daughter, without a trace of self-pity, maintaining her characteristic reserve.

Listen, said Elisa Vicuña: Chilean men, all Chilean men, speak softly, with a slightly feminine tone of voice, don't they? Whereas Argentinean men are always shouting out loud. I don't know what they've got in their throats, but they're like megaphones. Well, at first you can get the impression that all Argentinean men are super-virile, I mean, *we* can get that impression. But more careful and detailed observation reveals something else, almost the opposite, in fact. Haven't you noticed? Patri shrugged her shoulders. Her mother went on: Think of the architect who designed this building, and the decorators who come with the owners, all the men who came this morning, for example . . . Don't tell me you haven't noticed, Patricita: those pink silk cravats, the aftershave, those tank tops, the oohs! and ahs! In spite of everything that was on her mind, Patri couldn't help smiling at her mother's mimicry. Elisa went on:

Now there's another question, and it's closely related: the question of money. Having money is a kind of virility, *the only kind that counts in Argentina.* That's why this country we have come to is so unique and strange. That's why it has cut us off from the rest of the world, to which we belong by right as foreigners, and held us like hostages. It's true that there is, or at least should be, another form of virility, which doesn't depend on money. But where we are now, it's hard to imagine; as if, to understand it, we'd have to go back in time and space, back to Chile and even further, to something before that. What is that other form of virility? *Popular* virility? No, because the popular is subordinate; it's an eminently subordinate form in the hierarchy of virilities. It's the primitive form; that is, virility independent of the state. Although in principle it might seem preferable to the popular form, the primitive form can be dangerous for us too. It could imply that women are condemned to the primitive, to savagery. And wouldn't that be dangerous? Isn't the state, after all, a safeguard, a kind of guarantee, which stops us disappearing altogether, even if it relegates us to the bottom of the ladder? Women, said Patri, will never disappear. That, my girl, replied her mother vigorously, is precisely what's in doubt.

But what has all this got to do with ghosts? Patri asked her again.

Ah, ghosts . . . Well, what is a ghost? I've been talking about Argentinean men and Chilean men, but that was just to make it clearer, the way animals are used in fables. Well, so far it's not all that clear, said Patri. Come on, a smart girl like you . . . You see, for us there are always ghosts. Subtract a Chilean man from an Argentinean, or vice versa. Or add them up. You can actually do whatever you like. The result will always be the same: a ghost.

OK, but why do they have to be gay?

Even at that critical moment, when, as she was intuitively aware, her beloved daughter's life hung in the balance, Elisa Vicuña could not bring herself to answer with anything more than a mysterious smile, the "serious smile."

Since the coffee was ready, and a fragrant plume of steam was rising from the spout of the pot, they went back out. Patri put the tray on the table, and Inés Viñas took charge of filling each cup. The coffee was so well brewed, so aromatic, that hardly anyone felt the need to sweeten it. Patri took a sip, and waited for it to cool. She was thinking about the conversation with her mother just before: they hadn't come to any kind of conclusion; in fact, her doubts had multiplied. And yet the conversation had produced effects, and that was what she was thinking about as she drank her coffee. The danger, she thought, was not so much that the ghosts who were waiting for her would turn out to be a complete flop as far their virility was concerned, but that none of them would deign to talk to her, and give her the explanations she needed so badly. On second thought, however, the conversation had produced the opposite effect, since it was all about entering a state where she would no longer need anyone to look after her, or provide explanations, or even give her what her mom gave as abundantly as anyone could: love. And as she proceeded from this conclusion to a third stage in her reflections, the question of the ghosts' real virility recovered its importance. It might seem odd that this relatively uneducated young woman, who hadn't even finished secondary school, should entertain such elaborate thoughts. But it's not as strange as it seems. A person might never have thought at all, might have lived as a quivering bundle of futile, momentary passions, and yet at any moment, just like that, ideas as subtle as any that have ever occurred to the greatest philosophers might dawn on him or her. This seems utterly paradoxical, but in fact it happens every day. Thought is absorbed from others, who don't think either, but find their thoughts ready-made, and so on. This might seem to be a system spinning in a void, but not entirely; it is grounded, although it's hard to say just how. An example might clarify the point, though only in an analogical mode: imagine one of those people who don't think, a man whose only activity is reading novels, which for him is a purely pleasurable activity, and requires not the slightest intellectual effort; it's simply a matter of letting the pleasure of reading carry him along. Suddenly, some gesture or sentence, not to speak of a "thought," reveals that he is a philosopher in spite of himself. Where did he get that knowledge? From pleasure? From novels? An absurd supposition, given his reading material (if he read Thomas Mann, at least, it might be a different story). Knowledge comes *through* the novels, of course, but not really *from* them. They are not the ground; you couldn't expect them to be. They're suspended in the void, like everything else. But there they are, they exist: you can't say that it's a complete void. (With television, the argument would be harder to sustain.)

The guests were cracking jokes and laughing heartily as they drank their coffee and smoked cigarettes. They all gulped their cups down and asked if there was more. If I'd known you were going to like it so much I would have made a bigger pot, said Elisa Vicuña. Still, there was enough left to give a few people a smaller second cup. The children had started to agitate about the rockets, and since Javier, who was in charge of all the pyrotechnical gear, had told them to wait for the grown-ups, not even letting them have the lighter, they kept begging the adults to finish their coffee and come and help. All right, all right. The moon bathed them all in a marvelous whiteness, which even crept into the light globe's yellow glow. An atmosphere of carefree triviality reigned: keeping an eye on the time to see how many minutes were left, that sort of thing. The "real men" thought Patri, in her philosophical reverie, were none other than the men she could see before her now. And that was how it had to be, given everything her mother had been telling her for years. Elisa Vicuña's thoughts had not come out of nowhere, arbitrarily. They had come out of men, and gone in a circle, from men back to men, and that route made them "real" whether or not they really were. It was almost like getting used to something, anything, even this after-dinner banality. She started to think more carefully about the problem or the choice she was facing; she tried to put her thoughts in order.

Finally the parents agreed to oversee the lighting of the fireworks. Although it would have seemed impossible only a minute before, the level of excitement among the children rose abruptly. Roberto, who according to his girl-friend was a child at heart, was the keenest to join in, and to the amusement of all present, he even reached into his pocket and produced a sizeable supply of rockets, which he had brought "just in case." So they started with rockets, as well as jumping jacks and firecrackers. The explosions were lots of fun. They tried throwing a cracker into the pool, and the explosion resonated like a building collapsing. More! Come on! They wanted to make a much bigger din. But Javier suggested they fire off some tubes. They used an empty bottle as a launcher. Instead of choosing a distant constellation, they aimed straight at the moon. I think it'll make it, said Ernesto. Roberto had an excellent silver lighter, which allowed him to adjust the flame's intensity

as well as its length. Raúl Viñas called it a blowtorch. They
lit the first tube's fuse and waited. Miraculously, or because
it was well made (a rarity in recent times), it shot straight
up into the sky leaving a golden wake. This time they all
looked. It exploded way up high in a burst of very white
phosphorescence. The same thing happened with the second tube, except that the explosion was red, a dark, metallic
red. They had some very big, powerful fireworks, but they
were keeping them for later. The smaller children, Ernesto
and Jacqueline, were twirling sparklers.

The only one who wasn't taking part in the fun, or not
directly, was Patri, because she was busy thinking. It had
occurred to her that she didn't really have to wait to find
out, she could make a deductive leap: by deducing correctly
it was possible to tell what would happen. She couldn't
base her deductions on the ghosts, because she didn't know
anything about them. But she could use facial expressions
instead. She did her very best, calling on her imagination,
her unschooled—some might say naïve—creative gifts, but
she kept coming to the same conclusion: the mysterious
smile on the lips of the ghosts. It was inevitable, given her
skeptical nature: ending with a mysterious smile, like an
impenetrable barrier.

And what was the meaning of the mysterious smile?
She could deduce that too, but in reverse, since any of the
people here, the women sitting, the men crouching with
the children and playing with the rockets, any of the things
they might say or do, could provoke the mysterious smile.

It was within everyone's reach. So life in its entirety, with its infinite conclusions, was, it turned out, the deduction, the genealogy, of the mysterious smile.

While Raúl Viñas had gone off to refill his glass and drink it (which meant he would have to fill it again, but that was his business), Roberto and Javier put one of the really big rockets in a bottle to fire it off, and decided that in spite of the sparks, they would have to hold the bottle, using a napkin if need be to protect against burns, because it was so big and top-heavy it might fall over before take-off. So that was what they did; they brought Roberto's aerodynamic lighter up to the fuse, and shouted to get everyone's attention. Magnificently, triumphantly, trailing a dense wake or jet of sparks, the rocket shot up into the starry sky, crowded now with fireworks from every quarter of the city. As it went past the big parabolic dish, the glow lit up two ghosts floating in the night air, one perfectly vertical, the other at a slight angle, his head behind the head of his companion. That was the time: five to midnight, more or less. At midnight, they would be lined up perfectly, one behind the other, stuck together. Javier and Roberto smiled and whispered obscene remarks about that position; then almost immediately, prompted by the same association of ideas, they both looked at Patri, who was sitting very stiffly, staring into space, white as a sheet, cadaverous, so thin and haggard she could have been mistaken for a lifelike tailor's dummy.

Around her, the women were talking about New Year's resolutions, promises and hopes, which were sometimes indistinguishable. For Inés, it would be the pivotal year of her life, she said: the year of her marriage. The others agreed: afterward they would say "a year ago . . . two years ago . . . ten years ago"; it would be the milepost. And for Carmen, of course, the year would be marked by an event that was no less important for being repeated: the birth of a child. The years, they said, rolled on, and the children were the years, springing from the earth like capricious little butterflies, blown about by the breezes, by the days and weeks and months . . .

Suddenly the sirens blared. Midnight was imminent. The men rushed to light a string of rockets, which began to explode like joyous machine-gun fire. Before the volley was over, Patri got up and headed for the back of the terrace. Her step grew steadily quicker, although she didn't break into a run. All at once the others realized what she was intending to do; and far from being paralyzed by surprise, they got up in turn and went to stop her: the women, the men and the children, shouting out as rockets exploded near and far, and thousands of fireworks flowered in the sky. They didn't catch up with her, of course, although they came close. Patri leaped into the void. And that was it. The whole family came to a halt on the brink, right on the brink, and stood there speechless, as if their hearts, carried on by the momentum of the chase, had leaped as well. As she fell, Patri's thick glasses came off and went on falling separately, beside her. A ghost, appearing suddenly from somewhere, caught them safely before they hit the ground, and rose as if lifted by a gentle spring to the edge of the terrace, where he came to rest, in front of the family, who were stunned by the tragedy. He held the glasses out to Raúl Viñas, who reached out and took them. Man and ghost stared at each other.

13th of February 1987